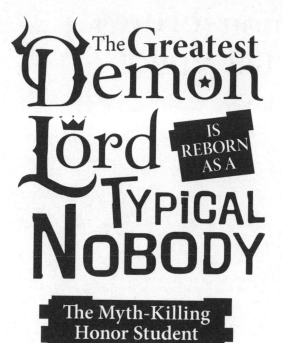

The Greatest Demon Lord IS REBORN AS A Typical Nobody

The Myth-Killing Honor Student

1

Myojin Katou
Illustration by **Sao Mizuno**

YEN ON

NEW YORK

The Greatest Demon Lord IS REBORN AS A Typical Nobody 1

Myojin Katou

Translation by Jessica Lange
Cover art by Sao Mizuno

SHIJOU SAIKYOU NO DAIMAOU, MURABITO A NI TENSEI SURU Volume 1 SHINWA GOROSHI NO YUUTOUSEI
©Myojin Katou, Sao Mizuno 2018
First published in Japan in 2018 by KADOKAWA CORPORATION, Tokyo.
English translation rights arranged with KADOKAWA CORPORATION, Tokyo through TUTTLE-MORI AGENCY, INC., Tokyo.

English translation © 2019 by Yen Press, LLC

Yen On
150 West 30th Street, 19th Floor
New York, NY 10001

Visit us at yenpress.com
facebook.com/yenpress
twitter.com/yenpress
yenpress.tumblr.com
instagram.com/yenpress

First Yen On Edition: November 2019

Yen On is an imprint of Yen Press, LLC.
The Yen On name and logo are trademarks of Yen Press, LLC.

Library of Congress Cataloging-in-Publication Data
Names: Katou, Myojin, author. | Mizuno, Sao, illustrator. | Lange, Jessica, translator.
Title: The greatest demon lord is reborn as a typical nobody / Myojin Katou ; illustration by Sao Mizuno ; translation by Jessica Lange.
Other titles: Shijou saikyou no daimaou, murabito a ni tensei suru. English
Description: First Yen On edition. | New York : Yen On, 2019.
Identifiers: LCCN 2019032131 | ISBN 9781975305680 (v. 1 ; trade paperback)
Subjects: CYAC: Fantasy. | Demonology—Fiction. | Reincarnation—Fiction.
Classification: LCC PZ7.1.K3726 Gr 2019 | DDC [Fic]—dc23
LC record available at https://lccn.loc.gov/2019032131

ISBNs: 978-1-9753-0568-0 (paperback)
       978-1-9753-0569-7 (ebook)

10 9 8 7 6 5 4 3 2 1

LSC-C

Printed in the United States of America

CONTENTS

The Greatest Demon Lord Is Reborn as a Typical Nobody
Myojin Katou
Illustration by Sao Mizuno

CHAPTER 1
The Lonely Demon Lord and His Rebirth in a New World

I want to experience defeat.

I don't even know when this thought first materialized in my mind, but I'd been going through life desperately clinging onto this wish.

I'd wasted most of my earlier days freeing humanity from divine beings and their devout followers. It seemed conflict trailed after my every move: Raise the army. Seize the country. Slaughter the heroes. Spread my influence. Exterminate the gods.

And by the time I'd reached the end of that journey, I was known as the "Demon Lord"—treated as though I was a monster straight out of a fairy tale. The general population and most of my underlings didn't see me as human but as an understudy for a god meant to be revered.

After all those years, I had only loneliness to show for my efforts, which was why I'd started to wish for my own defeat. If I pathetically fell to my knees, I figured someone would see me as human, too. At least, that'd been my line of thinking.

But my greatest wish was never to be fulfilled... There were no enemies left to defeat me.

It was inevitable that my life reach a checkmate. But I couldn't give it up.

In the end, I knew that the Demon Lord Varvatos would die a lonesome beast. He'd been born to carry this fate. But I could make up for it in my next life. I could chuckle in good company and live out my days in silly merriment as I'd done in the past. It was still possible.

When I couldn't bear the idea of spending another solitary moment, I'd scrambled to create a reincarnation spell and left a will behind for my underlings.

Then I'd let myself be whisked away.

...Yep. And now we're here. I was a brand-spankin'-new baby with tears rolling down my face.

With my brilliant technique, I'd reincarnated far off in the future as a *normal* human. I was no longer the Demon Lord Varvatos but Ard Meteor—just your average villager.

How time flies! I was six years old in the blink of an eye.

There wasn't much I could do in those years. And who could blame me? I was but a wee babe. I crawled forward, focusing on two things: acquiring language skills and amplifying my magical abilities. And that was the best I could manage. After all, I had the education and combat skills of your average kid, and I tried my best to whittle them into shape given the dire circumstances.

Which was why I hadn't made any friends.

Eh, I'm an average villager. I'm bound to make a friend or two at some point. I tried to laugh it off.

The seasons came and went, six years became ten...and I had yet to make a single friend.

But you've got to see that I couldn't do anything about it. That was the price I needed to pay in my pursuit of knowledge. I mean, we need to take in as much information as possible to live. Yeah, that sounds about right. I have to admit something: I wouldn't have been able to change this situation even if I'd tried.

Upon memorizing every last vocabulary word, I would lock myself away in my father's library, glued to books of all kinds and continuing to absorb the ways of this new era. You see, in life, wisdom trumps all else. I made the right choice holing up at home for all those years and reading books upon books upon books.

That day was just like any other. I'd trudged up to our home library to hunker down on the floor and read at my leisure. This wooden house was the kind you could find anywhere and was puny in comparison to my castle in my past life. But it was more than enough room for my parents and me.

I could feel the coolness of the floor against my butt as I turned the page of a history book.

"See? I told ya he'd be in here."

"You sure do love your books, Ard."

The door had been left ajar, and I could hear my parents chatting in front of it. My father's name was Jack, my mother's Carla, and both were human in every which way. Aside from being an attractive couple, they were perfectly normal villagers—nothing more, nothing less.

"Can I help you with something?" I asked.

"Nah, nothin' in particular."

If that's the case, I guess I'll continue reading.

...I'd somehow reincarnated three thousand years into the future. After my death, the world I'd unified slowly had dissolved into countless nations over the course of five hundred years. That paved the way for multiple periods of fierce power struggles, though it appeared the various peoples had achieved peace in the modern era.

That said, there was still evidence of demons wreaking havoc in the world. Or so I'd heard. It seemed they'd become more active as of late.

Apparently, a deity from a collective called the Outer Ones had been resurrected just ten years ago. They'd been my sworn enemies in ancient times and were better known as the "Evil Gods" in this era. It went without saying that this was an unprecedented calamity… And the ones who'd managed to save us all couldn't be considered standard by any means, either.

"The Great Mages and the Heroic Baron? Quite an impressive feat to take down an Evil God, especially with three people."

Even in my past life, I'd struggled to take on these deities. But these heroes had managed to do it with a team of three.

It was true that these were not your run-of-the-mill warriors, but the true reason for their strength must be the magical revolution that has taken place in this era, advancing the field of magic to incredible new heights. That was the only explanation that made sense. *After all, these gods aren't so weak that a handful of regular people can just take them out…*, was what I thought at the time.

"Well, well. Hee-hee-hee."

"Heh, looks like someone's shy."

The two were engrossed in an odd exchange that was totally beyond me, but I doubted it required my urgent attention.

I buried my nose back in my book.

How time flies! I'd turned twelve years old.

…Erm, friends? Yeah, none to speak of. I'd been meaning to make some—I swear. That's kind of the reason I'd reincarnated in the first place.

I'd finally thought about getting to know some other kids since I'd maxed out my pursuit of knowledge and all. But what do you know? I'm absolutely petrified of strangers, and I can't seem to strike up a conversation.

I know I'm not the Demon Lord anymore, but even if that's the case, I've come to learn that humans are organisms quick to reject strangers. What if someone shot me a look of *who the hell are you?*

or told me outright, *Yeesh, I don't wanna be friends with you?* The thought alone was more than enough to put me on edge, and I eventually lost my ability to even approach people, much less talk to them.

…Okay, fine. I confess. All that talk about training and the pursuit of knowledge yadda-yadda-yadda was an excuse. The truth is, I was tangled up in fear and anxiety, and it left me practically immobile.

Yeah, I was called the Demon Lord in my past life. Yeah, I'd never been intimidated by any gods. But now, a smattering of neighborhood children is all it takes to terrify me… I'm sure you can see how this wouldn't be "fine."

Sensing a crisis close at hand, I decided to ask those who'd mastered the relationship game for their tips and tricks. In other words, I went to my parents. I mean, they'd mated and given birth, right? From my perspective, that was enough to declare them successful at establishing friendships.

…Well then, take a look at my father's response: "Makin' friends? Ha-ha, that's easy! First, whoop them in the ass, then say, 'We're friends starting today!' and—"

"Isn't that how you make underlings?"

Cut to my mother's answer: "Hmm. Making friends… I know how to make sex slaves, but friends…"

"I'm sorry, what kind of life do you live, exactly?"

It seemed they weren't doing so hot on the social-acceptability scale.

When I finally realized I was looking in all the wrong places, I turned to Weiss—a handsome elven father and family friend of ours. He'd stayed at our house from time to time.

"I can't say I have a lot of friends…," he qualified, "but I think it would be good to show them you're a gentleman, you know. If you treat everyone with integrity and honesty, I'm sure you're bound to win someone over. And then you ask them to be your friend. Or something."

Weiss could teach my folks a thing or two.

With his advice in mind, I hurried off to put my friend-making plan into motion.

Another month came and went. But this time, the ex–Demon Lord was living out his days giggling and tagging along with his friends...

Not. That kind of crap was nowhere to be found.

That scene couldn't be further from the truth. For some inexplicable reason, people were actively avoiding me. I'd followed Weiss's advice to a T: I never forgot to smile; I always spoke politely to everyone; I made each and every gesture excessively elegant and refined.

And yet, no one wanted to strike up a friendship, much less come and approach me. Why the hell not?

Come to think of it, I'd heard a group of kids talking about me behind my back the other day.

"That Ard guy's pretty weird."

"Weird? Try creepy."

"Yeah, totally. Ew. Dude seriously gives me the heebie-jeebies."

It'd been a long time since I'd gotten the urge to destroy the world... Why did things have to turn out this way?

Another month for the books. Summertime. The days continued to be red-hot, but my attempts to connect with others remained ice-cold, stuck in the dead of winter.

And maybe it was from all this mental stress, but I sometimes caught myself crying for no reason and found a friggin' bald spot on the back of my head... I'm sure you can see how this wouldn't be "fine."

With the way things are going, maybe it's my destiny to be forever alone.

...I wasn't doing myself any favors by sulking, so I got ready to start my daily routine.

"Okay, Mother. I'm off."

"All righty! Take care, now!"

I left the house and trudged toward the mountain near the village. My goal? To practice magic.

The first thing I did was stamp down the foliage with my foot and elbow through the taller weeds to make my way up the mountain.

Well. Now that I'm here, it seems like today is a great day to take out my piss-poor relationship skills on some foliage, I thought when I heard a shrill scream.

"Aaaaaaaaagh!"

Based on that sound alone, I quickly surmised it was a girl.

But what would elicit such a cry in this peaceful mountain range? In any case, I figured I should hurry to the scene.

With the probing spell *Search* to pinpoint the target and teleportation spell *Dimension Walk* to transport my body to her location, I was instantly surrounded by a slight change of scenery.

"…Huh? Wh-where did you come from…?" sputtered a cute elven girl who was completely befuddled.

She was probably around my age and about a hundred and forty celti tall, which made her more than a full head shorter than I was. She was the epitome of beauty, and her features carried a lingering touch of cherubic innocence. Framing her head were locks of silver hair, sparkling like threads of the finest brocade under the sunlight, which filtered through the canopy of branches. Her hair reached down far enough to brush against her knees, and the ends were tied off daintily with ribbons.

"Graaaaaaaah!"

As I took in the sight, I saw the source of her distress from the corner of my eye. Unleashing a fierce howl was a giant wolf—large enough to make you crane your head to get a good look. Its bloodshot eyes zeroed in on us as its fur bristled, radiating pure hostility all the while.

"R-run away! I'll hold it back!" The girl with silver hair sprang out to shield me and draw its attention.

It was as if *she* was the one saving some damsel in distress from a big, scary monster.

"Um, excuse me. A word?" I asked politely.

"Wh-wh-wh-what?! I—I—I—I told you to run!"

"But…can I ask why you're so afraid? It's just a mutt."

"Wha—?! J-just a mutt?! Do you even hear yourself?!"

"Sure I do. I'm only telling you the truth."

The wolf interrupted our conversation with a low growl…then pounced toward her, just as I shoved her out of the way and unleashed a spell.

With my left palm extended toward the dog, I summoned a magic circle at the tips of my fingers to shoot out flames—swallowing the creature in a split second and incinerating it whole. A few seconds later, the charbroiled wolf fell over with a heavy *thud*.

The girl began to chatter on excitedly. "…Y-you took down an Ancient Wolf in one hit?! *And* cast *Mega Flare* without chanting?!"

What's with that reaction? I didn't do anything worth getting worked up over. Plus, "Ancient Wolf"? That mutt? Yeah, right.

I mean, Ancient Wolves were monsters that inhabited the deadly belt of trees and the home of mighty spirits, the Holy Forest. There's no way you'd find one anywhere near here, and they were actually strong, compared to ol' Fido over there.

There was one more thing she had gotten twisted.

"I used regular *Flare*, not *Mega Flare*, you know."

"…I'm sorry?"

Again, why was she so surprised? Did she really just mistake that move for *Mega Flare*? Seriously? Like, *Mega Flare*'s on a whole different level compared to your average *Flare*. The former was a mid-level fire spell, capable of roasting hundreds of people, and the latter was elementary level at best. There was no way anyone could mistake one for the other.

"…Y-yeah, you're right! G-guess it was just a slip of the tongue! Ah-ha-ha-ha!" She blew it off with a guffaw, though it seemed suspiciously forced.

Then she looked up at me with her big eyes. "A-anyway! Y-you got a name, mister?!"

"I go by Ard Meteor. It's a pleasure to make your acquaintance."

"I—I see. I'm Ireena…" Her fidgeting caused her thighs to rub against each other as she nervously thrust out a hand.

"I-I-I-I'll let you be my first friend!"

I couldn't help but stare at the hand before me. This sudden development had me frozen in place, and when I finally calmed down enough to assess the situation…I was overcome by a fervent jubilation that swelled in my heart.

"…If that is what you wish, I'll be your friend forevermore."

The moment I gripped her hand, Ireena's entire body gave a jolt and began to tremble. A few seconds later, she pinched her face with both hands while wearing an expression that had *Is this for real? I'm not dreaming, am I?* plastered all over it.

Then her mouth broke into a smile from ear to ear on her charming little face. It was honestly as bright as the sun.

Gazing upon it, I felt a certain nostalgia… This girl reminded me of someone I used to know: the one and only friend I'd had and lost in my past life. For a moment, it was as if we'd been reunited, and I couldn't help but smile back in response.

"Oh, by the way, Ireena. You may want to reevaluate whether you should extend your left hand in greeting."

"What?! I-is it bad?!"

"Yeah. Using your left hand means...and if you'll pardon my forwardness...'You dirty bastard, I'm going to friggin' murder you!'"

"*What?!* N-no, I...I never meant it like that! I'm sorry!"

Oh, Ireena. She stood around looking all flustered and cute. It felt less like I'd made a friend—and more like she was my daughter.

CHAPTER 2
The Ex–Demon Lord on Top of the World with His New Friend

For a long time, I'd been troubled by my lack of friends, when an opportunity came knocking on my door.

Yeah, I'm talking about Ireena... Though if I'm being completely honest, everything happened so fast that it still hasn't really sunk in yet. But, eh, I guess new friendships can be that way sometimes. Not that I know from personal experience. In any case, I had a little pep to my step ever since our first encounter, and my days were filled with exploring the mountains together and splashing water on each other and sharing a bed and on and on and on... I was seriously blessed.

Before our chance encounter, I'd been slinking around beset by a lingering sense of loneliness, which had trailed after me from my previous life into this one. But now, it'd completely dissipated, leaving my heart with nothing but boundless joy.

On this day, I continued to act out the part of a healthy child, thinking about my plans to chase Ireena through some fields as I waited for her to arrive at my house, just past noon...

"Hi-ho, Ard! Lookie what I got! Yahoo!"

It wasn't Ireena who'd entered my room but my gratingly hyperactive father, brandishing a long sword with an exquisite blade winking under the light.

"My old sword was lookin' pretty shabby, so I splurged on a new one!" My father continued to squeal and squirm around in excitement. Looking at him made me sick, if I was being honest.

"Look here, Ardy-Ard! *Super*cool, ain't it? Top-quality stuff!" He thrust it in my direction, keeping up his irritatingly cheery act.

I gripped the hilt and stared at the blade. "Father. It pains me to inform you that you've been scammed. This sword is worthless."

He tilted his head and let out a pathetic "Whaaaaaat?" It seemed he didn't have a very discerning eye.

"I mean, this blade has a *Sharpness* level of ten. A half-hearted attempt at best. Given the quality of the sword, it should be able to hold three attributes if the proper compression techniques are used."

"...Wha—? No, wait, that's... Huh?" My father stared blankly at me.

I bet he was shocked to find out that he'd been bamboozled into buying a piece of junk.

"But there's no need to worry. It's possible to refine it into a normal sword, though I can't say it'll be top quality." I invested my power into the sword before handing it back to him.

"Right... Just curious. What attributes did ya give it?"

"A *Sharpness* level of one hundred. *Fire Support. Self-Sharpening Blade.* And that's about it."

As soon as I answered, he swung the sword at a desk nearby and sliced off a corner, engulfing it in flames and turning it to ash before it had a chance to hit the floor, thanks to *Fire Support.* Oh yikes. He must be pissed off that he'd been deceived, and I guess I couldn't blame him for taking it out on an inanimate object. I mean, you should have seen the blade before.

"...You've gotta be kidding me," he mumbled to himself as he gazed at it.

Yeesh, I bet he's seething. At this rate, he'll beat the shit out of the old man running the smithy—

"Arrrrd! I'm heeere!"

Welp, that's not any of my business. Best to let him do as he pleases. Plus, my day was all booked, since I'd be busy frolicking with Ireena. All other plans could get to the back of the line.

I rushed over to the door, abandoning my hot-tempered father in the room.

"I'm sorry to have kept you waiting."

"Not at all! C'mon, let's go!" Ireena grabbed my hand and yanked me outside, energetically trotting along next to me and looking as cute as always.

That lovely silver hair. Her doll-like face. That milky, almost porcelain skin. And her chest peeking through her sheer white dress.

Plus, cleavage.

Also, side boobs.

I'd never felt luckier to be her friend.

We managed to make it to the mountains.

"Oh, I almost forgot. Daddy says he wants to make a new sword and asked me to gather materials for it... Could you help me?"

"Why, of course. What might you be searching for?"

"Hmm... I think we need two fangs from an Ultima Tiger, some body fluid from a Meteo Slime, and a magic stone from an Ancient Boa."

I hate to inform you that there's no way we'll find any of those on this mountain. I mean, every single item on that list would be found only in destinations for the most daring of adventurers. I bet this was her dad's idea of a joke, but it was easy enough to figure out which monsters were close enough to what he was actually looking for—give or take a few qualities—and then hunt those down.

After we'd managed to wrap that up in record time, we mixed work and play by "grinding," which involved hunting every beast we could find in a nearby dungeon for experience points. I could feel my magical energy increase in fractional increments as I took them down one by one. This was the fastest way to become a master mage.

We holed up and farmed monsters for five hours before ducking out of the dungeon. I was still pumped and raring to go, but Ireena was completely exhausted. We took a short break outside, and she'd just started to recover from her fatigue when she suddenly looked up at me.

"H-hey, Ard. I've been, you know... I wanna learn how to cast a spell without an incantation!" she demanded.

"Well, that's surprising. Weren't you the one who told me you'd mastered it when you were three?"

"Th-that... So what? That was then! And this is now!" she yelped, her face burning red and eyes growing dewy with tears.

Judging by her reaction, it was clear she had been lying.

Huh, so she really can't do it.

"Well, okay. Fine. But before we begin...tell me: What is magic?"

"Heh-heh-heh! Easy peasy! Magic comes from the language of runes created by the Demon Lord! And by reciting the chants recorded in these symbols, we can unleash spells! The whole reaction is powered by consuming our own magical energy! That's what magic is!"

She eagerly glanced in my direction, her face an open book: *I'm right, aren't I? You know you can praise me, right? C'mon, please! Woof, woof!*

I obliged, stroking her head.

"Hee-hee-hee...! W-well, I'm the best, after all! Nothin' to it!"

she tooted, puffing out her chest all triumphantly. *Geez, she's so friggin' cute.*

"Well then, Ireena. What's an incantion? Why must we use runes? What's the connection between runes and spells?"

These questions caught her off guard—but I'd expected that, since our textbooks didn't cover them. Well, it'd be more accurate to say that our books only contained information about lower-level spells, which were super weak compared to equivalent techniques in my past life.

I bet someone put these preventative measures in place to keep the masses from gaining too much power. I'd heard our policy makers weren't too keen on sharing. My best guess was that they were terrified of the commoners. Especially considering how the most accessible spells were weak as shit, I could only assume the nobility had siphoned off all the best techniques for themselves and passed them down among themselves from generation to generation.

"Listen carefully, Ireena. Magic depends on the composition of a magic circle."

"Composition of a…magic circle?"

"That's correct. When we recite a chant, we're creating a magic circle by reading aloud its contents, which we call the magical formula. That causes the circle to fill with magical energy. This is one part of how we cast magic."

Holding up my index finger, I continued on. "It's perfectly possible to form a magic circle without a chant by projecting a clear image of it in your mind."

To drive my explanation home, I summoned one at my fingertips to invoke *Flare* in front of Ireena. "Try to call forth magic while you visualize it in your mind."

"G-got it!" Ireena nodded as she thrust her palm toward the heavens, and a small burst of fire sputtered out of her magic circle.

"Wowie! Wow, wow, wow! I did it! Bye-bye, chanting!"

Oh god, her innocent delight made her extra cute and warmed my heart just by looking at her.

"I did it! I did it! Hooray!" she squealed, casting magic over and over in absolute joy.

As I watched this tender moment, I couldn't help but feel slightly blue. You see, the power and effectiveness of a magic circle widely varied, depending on how much magical energy was consumed. To make things simple, if a normal *Flare* spell takes one hundred units to execute...then Ireena's was at twenty, which made her magic dismally weak. I would've bet that her magical energy was much lower than average.

In other words, she had zero talent. It would probably break her heart when she found that out in the future.

"I did it! Look at me go! We're on the same level now, Ard!"

...But I'd already decided I would always support this silly girl, no questions asked. I'd take on her burdens as my own—her sorrows, her pain, everything—and pull her to her feet every time she failed.

Because that's the true meaning of friendship.

Time flew by with Ireena (my sweet baby angel) by my side. With a sprinkling of this and a smattering of that, I'd managed to turn fifteen years old.

As in my past life, this was the age of full-fledged adulthood. Around this time, people started to map out the rest of their lives and seriously contemplated their future occupations. It went without saying that both of our parents were well aware of that fact.

On this evening, Ireena and her father were to join my family for a roundtable about our futures. It was around nine in the evening when the sky was cloaked in an inky darkness, and a flaxen moon lit my surroundings. A concert of chirping insects serenaded those who passed.

There was a knock at the door, and I went to greet our guests in my parents' place.

"Gooooood evening, Ard!" It was Ireena, whose abounding cheerfulness never set with the sun.

"Hello there, Ard. Good evening," greeted her white-haired elven father, Weiss.

I ushered them inside to get everyone seated at the dining table, where we first offered a prayer before digging in.

"We thank our Father—the Demon Lord Varvatos—and Her Majesty the Queen for this bounty."

In this time period, it seemed that a religion with me as the chief deity had taken root. The entire world worshipped me, but I had… very mixed feelings, as you can imagine. Leaving the whole "Queen" part aside, why did they have to offer me thanks in the first place?

"Okay, now that we got this dumb prayer out of the way, go ahead and chow down! Ard's curry is just as delicious today as any other day!"

"Yaaaay! Thanks for the food!" Ireena started to gulp it down in a hurry.

Geez, even her gluttony's starting to look all cutesy.

"Tee-hee. As adorable as ever, Ireena. A striking image of your mother… Ahhh, I want to have so much *fun* with you…," my mother moaned, spouting out some seriously criminal comments with a lewd expression on her face.

Paying no attention to this predator, Ireena continued to dig in.

…Incidentally, I didn't know the details about her mother, but considering she'd never joined us for dinner, I could probably venture a guess.

Well, thanks to Ireena, I enjoyed my dinner very much.

"Why don't we get started?" Weiss placed his spoon on the table and cut to the heart of the matter. His androgynous beauty was highlighted by a soft smile, but his eyes shone with solemn determination. "First up: Ard. What would you like to do?"

"Yes, well… There are a number of things, but at the moment…I'd like to make a hundred friends."

"Ha-ha-ha. I have to admit, I've never been able to tell what you're thinking," he said, inexplicably chuckling before turning to Ireena. "And what about you? *The crux of your future has already been decided*, but there's still some time before then. What do you think you'll do?"

"Hmm… Well, for now… I—I think I want to be with Ard. Yeah," she whispered as she shyly scratched at her blushing cheeks and cast her eyes down.

Gah! She was honestly just too precious.

"Right. I understand both your feelings. I have the perfect solution."

"I reckon it'd be best for you both to attend the Academy of Magic."

"It's perfect for your goal, Ard, and I'm sure it'll help your dreams come true, too, Ireena!"

Hearing the word *academy* sent a wave of pain rippling through my stomach. I mean, sure, it'd be the fastest way to make friends. In fact, I'd had that exact same idea in my former life when I'd transformed myself into your average Joe, lying about my past to enter an academy. It was the best solution I could think up: hide my true form and live as someone else to make some friends but…I'd managed to remain alone and in isolation despite my foolproof plan. Amazing.

And, well, if I'm being perfectly honest here, I was bullied—hard.

Imagine this: the Demon Lord suffering at the hands of the lowly commoners.

Like, for example, there was this one time when I left class to take care of some business in the bathroom, as you do, and they nicknamed me the "poop man" and made me into a laughingstock! And they even went so far as to scribble on my desk and dirty my textbooks... I ended up quitting school after a year. I'm sure you can see how I've associated academies with a boatload of trauma.

"The Academy of Magic?! Wowie! That sounds super fun!" Ireena's eyes sparkled.

I couldn't possibly say I didn't want to go with her, god forbid. I mean, come on. That smile. I needed to protect it.

"I have no objections. I'll join Ireena and enter the academy."

"Great. For the best, I'm sure. And I bet you'll be able to make plenty of friends... Oh, and, Ard, I think it'll be a good chance to readjust your common-sense compass."

Common sense? I had more common sense than anyone. I mean, I was once the great Demon Lord. I wouldn't have been able to navigate diplomatic solutions and conduct other official business if I hadn't excelled in every conceivable aspect of common knowledge and etiquette.

Well, Weiss was probably just trying to say I was still a child. Made sense. I nodded obediently...and promptly changed the subject.

"I'm fine and well with enrolling in the academy, but do we meet their qualifications?"

"Hmm? Qualifications?"

"I realize I know very little about the academy, but...do they accept commoners? I was under the impression that it's an institution designed to serve the nobility."

"No need to worry. Sure, the nobles used to discriminate against the commoners way back when, and we couldn't afford the tuition, much less attend the school. But in recent years, its doors are open to everyone... But that's beside the point. There's no place that's closed off to either of you."

"—? What do you mean by that?" I tilted my head in a gesture of confusion, which Weiss returned in kind.

"...Hey, you guys. Haven't you told this kid anything?" he asked, giving my parents a look.

"Ah, well, y'know. I like *hearing* tales of derring-do, too, but..."

"We don't like talking about ourselves much. It's so embarrassing."

My parents gave a nervous chuckle, and Weiss sighed, turning his gaze back to me.

"Listen up, Ard. What I'm about to tell you is the full and honest truth."

And then...he hit me with a surprising revelation.

"Your parents are the renowned Great Mages, and I'm the Heroic Baron, though it feels kind of cheesy to call myself that. In short, all three of us are off the charts in terms of strength."

"What?" I spilled out pathetically before I had a chance to stop it from leaving my lips. This was way too much to take in, but I could tell Weiss was dead serious. There was no question that what he was saying was the truth.

...To be honest, I had a few hang-ups about this entire situation.

I refused to be set apart. I despised it to the extent that it made me recoil in disgust to see myself get so worked up. In my past life, I'd lost so much for being the Demon Lord, for being "special." You see, uniqueness and loneliness were merely two sides of the same coin, and I knew that all too well, which was why I hated standing out and avoided it to the best of my ability.

But what's done is done. I'd begrudgingly accept that I was the son of the Great Mages. Plus, it seemed they were mutants, fortunately, according to the texts. In general terms, it meant they were born with exceptional abilities that went beyond the limits of their species. But these qualities weren't hereditary, which meant they came and went with their birth and death. This was my saving grace: My parents might be special, but I wasn't any different from others. I'd never be known as the Demon Lord again.

The meeting carried on and ended without dispute. When the meal was almost done, Weiss looked at me with a serious expression.

"…I'm trusting you to look after Ireena at the academy, Ard."

Just your typical parental speech. But there was something that caught my attention.

Why did Weiss's face harbor so much fear and anxiety?

CHAPTER 3
The Ex–Demon Lord and His Mission to Make One Hundred Friends

A week later, Ireena and I said farewell to our parents and boarded a carriage. The trip to the royal capital of Dycaeus took a few days.

When we arrived, I instantly noticed the place was markedly different from my past life. I guess that was to be expected. First things first, there wasn't a single wall or gate in sight. Back in my day, we'd all agreed that the capital needed to be fortified to the max, but this era clearly had other ideas. That, or this city was out of its mind. It seriously looked like a bustling cityscape had been chucked into an open field and left there without any thought to military defense. The whole concept was novel to me.

Anyway, after we reached the drop-off zone near the entrance and thanked the coachman, the two of us took in the royal capital in all its glory.

"My… This certainly is splendid."

It was as though I'd entered another world altogether: The capital was nothing like our village back home. There was a smattering of stone and brick structures, which I'd become well acquainted with, but most of the buildings were constructed in unfathomable ways using mystifying materials. I would've lost my mind if I'd seen some ginormous buildings piercing the sky above me back in my day.

This was the best part of reincarnation, as cliché as that sounded.

With that said, it wasn't as if we could stand around taking in the scenery forever. Our next engagement involved meeting with the head of the academy, which wasn't exactly something we could bail on. We lined up side by side and set out, weaving through the main street. It was bustling with activity and buildings sandwiched tightly on either side of the cobblestone road, where people sauntered on. We made our way to the academy at a leisurely stroll. Peace at last.

...Well, except for the constant flood of vulgar gazes directed at Ireena.

"Hey, that chick's hella cute... Dare me to talk to her?"

"Give it up, dude. She's wearing the uniform of the academy. I bet she's a noble or rich."

"Geez, she's way outta my league."

Those scumbags had one thing right: We were both in uniform, even though we hadn't officially enrolled at the school yet. They were sent for us to wear as students, even though our admission was technically up in the air and contingent on a few things. Nothing about my uniform was worth mentioning, but Ireena's was...*very* revealing to say the least.

Thanks to this crafty design, Ireena's thick thighs and shapely breasts were on full display. Coupled with her irresistible good looks, she made twelve out of every ten people do a double take.

"Heh-heh-heh, they can't get enough of me!"

"It's inevitable. Your beauty will always turn heads, Ireena."

I was prim and proper on the surface, but I seethed with anger internally. Anyone who directed their carnal desires at my sweet daughter would face certain death for their sins.

Maybe I should get half-naked and redirect their attention.

I was just about ready to seriously put this plan into action.

"Shaddup! All I did was kill some dumb stray cat!" sneered a dicey voice that caused us to stop in our tracks.

I *knew* this would cause me to get tangled up in some annoying mess, but I humored them and turned toward the source. By a wall in the corner of the main street, some orc boys were looming over...a beautiful girl who looked around eighteen.

Since she didn't have any bodily characteristics or auras that suggested otherwise, I surmised she was a human. In any case, her appearance immediately caught my attention. Her features were delicate as a doll's and framed with long platinum-blond locks. She looked absolutely divine.

"...Well, I think you lot are worth way less than that 'dumb stray cat.'"

"*What?!* Just try and say that again!" bellowed an orc in a murderous fit.

...They were so far gone that I wouldn't be able to deescalate the situation by talking.

"I have to help her!" Ireena yelped, trying to rush to the scene, but I held her back.

"Please wait, Ireena. You spectate. I shall see to it."

As my dear friend and student, she had to know the rules of combat. That said, she wasn't exactly at the level where she could take on a group of orcs. Especially since they were known to be stubborn. Which left me with one option: It was time for this humble ex-Demon-Lord-turned-villager to make his entrance.

Ireena complied, and I made my way toward the group—smashing a nearby orc in the back of the head with a one-hit KO. The color drained from the faces of the rest of the group at this surprise attack. Spotting an opportunity, I swiftly turned to take out the rest.

Palm strike to chin. Front kick to groin.

Two down in one blow. The remaining three lined up before me.

"Who the hell are you?!" one screeched.

They lumbered over, fueled by rage and readying themselves as they closed in…but I rushed toward them, closing the distance between us in an instant, and bashed each head in succession. They toppled to the ground in a crumpled heap.

"How rude," I spat curtly before turning to the girl. "Are you all right, my lady?"

She blinked in momentary surprise. "Yeah, all thanks to you. Those were some pretty impressive moves just now," she commented with a grin.

Ireena chimed in. "I know, right?! Isn't he so cool?! And here is my friend, y'know!" she blubbered excitedly as if she'd been the one praised by this stranger. Ireena's totally an angel.

"Yeah, it really was something else. I mean, not just anyone can cast buffing magic. I couldn't help but cheer on as I watched you take 'em down—"

"I'm sorry, but that altercation involved no magic whatsoever."

"What? …You must be kidding. You're human, aren't you? A human couldn't possibly take down an orc with his bare hands," she blurted out with a clueless expression stuck on her face.

I smiled and shook my head. "It's all about how, where, and when you strike. Once you know that, it's simple."

"B-but, uh, the way you rushed in? I mean, you moved faster than a human can."

"Another clever trick. I could tell these amateurs had no understanding of magic. I thought it'd be overkill to cast a spell on them, which was why I chose to engage them in hand-to-hand combat."

"I see…" The girl's eyes narrowed.

I shivered as a chill ran down my spine.

What's going on? There shouldn't have been any reason she'd make me feel this way.

As my suspicions about her mounted, she violently thumped me on the back. "Ha-ha-ha, you're a wild one, huh? I like you!"

Soon enough, she changed the subject. "By the way, you two. Those uniforms. Are you students at the Academy of Magic?"

"I'm afraid not. I haven't enrolled yet. Same goes for Ireena over here."

"Hmm. Ah, come to think of it, I heard there might be two students with contingent admission joining this year. Must be you guys. In that case, I doubt we'll hear any complaints."

"…Are you connected with the academy in some way?"

"That's right. I'll be an instructor this year. The youngest in its history," she boasted, flashing us a triumphant look that clearly said, *Whaddaya think of that?*

"I'm Jessica. Jessica von Velgr la Melldies de Rainsworth. I'm the third daughter of a marquis, but no need to act all formally with me, y'hear?" She flashed us a cheery smile and stuck her hand out assertively.

I accepted it, and we introduced ourselves in return.

"Ard and Ireena, huh? Well, I've got business at the academy, too. Why don't we all head over together?"

We strolled alongside one another to our destination and passed through the gates into the grounds proper. The Laville National Academy of Magic was the largest school in the country, and it had a cutting-edge curriculum. Its grounds stretched out farther than its outer appearance let on… And to be honest, the sprawling campus overwhelmed the two of us.

Jessica giggled. "Give it three days, and it'll feel like old news… Well, I've gotta go to the staff room, so this is where we part ways. Next time we meet, we'll be teacher and students."

With this lighthearted farewell, she waved at us and took her leave.

After Jessica departed, we cornered a few students on campus as we tried to figure out our way to the headmaster's office. As we meandered across the grounds, I noticed two variations of our uniform, which signified status. Based on this info, I bet there were remnants of a social hierarchy that separated the rich from the poor.

I mulled this over while traveling through the school building with Ireena until we finally arrived at the door to the office, on which I gave a few quick raps with my knuckle before entering.

"Oh, you've made it. Thank you for coming," croaked the headmaster, an elderly man named Golde, as he ushered us in congenially and assumed his position in front of a desk smack-dab in the center of the spacious room.

He looked like he couldn't have been more than a couple days away from hitting one hundred, but he overflowed with a vitality that belied his appearance. He was a count and held the sixth position of mageship, known as "Hexagon"—only one rank away from the very top. There were fewer than ten people who'd earned this title throughout the nation. It wouldn't be possible for an average villager (read: me) to be bestowed with this honor, though that wouldn't have been the case back in my heyday.

Next to Count Golde was an attractive young woman. I guessed she was his secretary or something. She'd kept silent until now, staring daggers in our direction.

"...As expected from those three. Irregular, indeed. Like parent, like child," she muttered quietly.

This woman was a piss-poor judge of character. What about us was *irregular*?

"Ooh, yes, quite fearsome. It seems they'll do much better than we've been told."

...Apparently, the count needed to get his eyes checked, stat, especially if he was expecting something from a normal village boy and a less-than-mediocre girl.

"We've heard of your heroism. You will be exempt from the practical exams. There's no question you'd receive full marks. Especially you, Ard. If you were to go up against an exam proctor, he'd die if he wasn't careful. Yes, indeed. Such frightening talent."

It was all lip service. And I had nothing to do with it. Our parents were renowned as some of the greatest heroes in history, so the academy could hardly afford to flat-out reject their kids.

"However. We ask that you take the written exam. I think it'll be an easy enough task for you both, but…I'm afraid I cannot allow you to enroll otherwise."

Gotcha. That'll test our basic education. They could never allow two uneducated students into their school. We both nodded obediently.

"Very good… It's a bit preemptive, but perhaps I should say it now. Welcome to the Laville National Academy of Magic. I'm honored to have you here with us."

Sheesh, talk about overkill. Ireena and I were perfectly average.

Well, probably less than average.

A few days later, I was right in the middle of scribbling through the written examination at the academy, joined by a few other students.

…Weird. Totally bonkers. The test is way too easy. This must be what they call a trick question, I bet.

It had to be one of those problems where you squeeze out an answer by reading between the lines and words and spaces. Yeah. That had to be it. I mean, otherwise a three-year-old could pass with flying colors.

It was obvious. After all, this academy stood at the forefront of all other institutions in the country, founded during the earliest days of the nation to provide a well-rounded education.

Makes sense that they'll have some tricky problems on their test. Nice. This is gonna be fun.

On the morning after the exam, I headed to the academy with Ireena in tow.

The results were posted on a signboard at the front gate, swarming with a crowd of students—smiling or sobbing in typical post-exam fashion.

"Well! There's obviously no way *we'll* fail! We're gonna knock this one outta the park!" Ireena powered forward, her chest swelling with confidence.

I trailed after her and took a good look at the results.

It didn't take long to confirm that we'd gotten in. After all, both our names were at the very top of the list. Ireena scored full points. Amazing. My darling little girl was so smart.

I, on the other hand…

"Hey. Hey, Ard. Doesn't this seem strange?"

"I-indeed. I don't understand it, either," I said, bewildered.

It made no sense. I'd scored a grand total of…zero points.

CHAPTER 4
The Ex–Demon Lord Reunited with Trouble

I looked and looked again at the score in front of me, which remained a zero each time. But I was still listed as the top-ranking score.

What does this mean? Also, the test was apparently out of ten billion points, which had been written next to the big, fat zero. What the hell was this all about?

Ireena and I were at a total loss, cocking our heads to the side in absolute confusion, when we heard a familiar voice.

"Hey there, you guys. Congrats on getting in!" chirped a platinum blonde, Jessica, grinning and standing in a crowd of test takers overcome with joy—or sorrow.

She called me over. "Come with me. The headmaster will explain your score."

We followed her lead to his office, where Golde greeted us the moment we stepped through a door.

"Ard! You're a genius! No, more than a genius! An absolute monster! No, even greater! A god! Yes, you're a *god*!" Count Golde bombarded me with accolades.

"…I'm sorry. I'm afraid I don't understand what you're saying."

"Ah, yes. *Ahem*. Sorry for acting so childish and getting all riled up," he replied sheepishly, scratching his head in embarrassment. "About your score," he started.

"Yes, a zero. I don't want to come across as rude, but I wasn't expecting that."

"Hmm… I want to ask you something. What compelled you to write those answers?"

"I thought the questions were too easy and assumed they were trying to trick me."

"'Too easy,' huh. I'll have you know, our exam is infamous for having the most challenging questions worldwide," Golde added with a wry smile.

I tilted my head. *The most challenging exam? Really? Even a toddler could pass it.*

"Well, in any case, you got every single question wrong. Your answers went…far beyond the correct ones." His eyes began to sparkle once again. "How did you come up with these answers? I've never even heard of someone using a magic-amplification circuit to make magic circles! And your idea to rearrange these techniques is godlike—divine! Even if I lived several hundred more years, I wouldn't be able to come up with that!" he exclaimed, reaching a fever pitch.

Golde wrapped up his little speech. "You might have scored a zero. But as a thesis on magic theory, this gets full points! No, more than that! These thoughts of yours would rock the entire world if we presented them to academic circles! They have the potential to alter history! You've ranked far beyond your fellow students, Ard! Take up a teaching position! Guide us as both student and teacher!"

He grabbed my hands and looked at me pleadingly with tears in his eyes… Why was he saying all of this? I was supposed to be a painfully average villager… Well, whatever.

"Heh-heh-heh! That's right! Ard is totally amazing! He's my friend *and* teacher! No one in this whole wide world is more awesome than he is!" Ireena smiled ecstatically, blasting away all my fears, which were trivial anyway.

And what could I say? Ireena was seriously the cutest person ever.

We moved into the student dorms immediately afterward and settled in. The following day, we attended the entrance ceremony.

Though it's customary for the top student of the new class to deliver a speech at the ceremony, I was thankfully spared from this duty. I knew more than anyone else that conformity was the best cure for the odd one out. Nothing good ever came from being the black sheep, that's for sure. And plus, if I wasn't careful, I'd end up getting bullied all over again.

But Ireena wasn't having any of it.

"Why didn't they ask you to go onstage, Ard...?! I wanted to see you up there in all your glory...!" she grumbled next to me.

I redirected my attention to the ceremony: The gorgeous student council president delivered the opening speech, followed by the heads of the four duchies, and on, and on... A real snore, if I'm being honest. Ireena started nodding off in the middle of it.

Right before the ceremony ended, the headmaster went up to the podium to deliver his final words.

"Well. You've all managed to conquer the grueling exam, rising to the top as the chosen few... But you mustn't forget that you're still baby chicks from our perspective. Remain diligent in your studies and stay humble."

Right on, Golde. We're practically newborns in this respect. I was on the same page as the headmaster for once. Right, I'd be prudent and study with—

"That said, there is one exception: a lion among you—a god on earth. Yes, we're blessed to observe this genius up close! Feast your eyes on this historic moment."

…Wait, what? Hold up. What the hell are you on? And why are you looking at me?

"Heh-heh-heh! Yes! Good one, Golde!"

Um, hello, Ireena? What are you getting all excited for—?

"Let's go, Ard! It's our time to shine!"

"Wha—?!" I yelped as she yanked my arm and dragged me to the podium, where Golde placed a hand on my shoulder.

"And his name is Ard Meteor! This girl over here is Ireena Litz de Olhyde! I'm sure you know what this means!"

Golde's comment created a stir: "Meteor?" "Olhyde?" "Hey, it can't be they're…" "Y-you're kidding!"

"Yes! These are the children of our heroes!" he roared.

"S-seriously?!"

"The child of the Great Mages?!"

"I—I never imagined I'd study alongside their kin…!"

It seemed our parents were highly revered, considering how this was enough for some students to tremble with joy or weep or faint from delirium… At least that was how the commoners reacted. The noble students were less enthusiastic.

"Yeah, yeah, the Great Mages? Peasants."

"How dare these commoners look down on us…!"

Oh, yikes. This is real bad.

As a simple villager, I wouldn't be able to deflect any new bullies, much less get payback when I dropped out of school again. And now that I'd been thrown into the wild, one part of the student body was all too quickly marking me as their newest enemy. At this rate, my reincarnation would end up completely pointless.

I turned to Golde as I started to feel danger creeping up my spine.

"U-um? I-I'd appreciate it if you'd stop—"

"Yessiree, this young man is a true genius! He's not like the rest of you! I mean, compared to him, you're…hmm…boogers! Yes! Snot! In conclusion, you should all aspire to reach his level and devote yourselves to your studies!"

This only escalated the situation.

"Hey, let's call one of the upperclassmen, like Raile, and get him to join in the brainiac hunt."

"Nah, Ma's better for these things, right?"

"Whatever. This 'Ard' character is on our hit list either way."

I was done for. Old news. Totally doomed. My school life had started and ended with the entrance ceremony. As I stood amid the turmoil Golde had wrought, I thought to myself: *Why did things turn out this way?*

They broke us up into our classes after the ceremony, and Ireena and I were assigned to the same class. We were all herded by the instructors to our respective rooms, where we waited for the homeroom teacher to arrive…and where the two of us were swarmed by hordes of students.

Ireena had captured the boys' attention, while I was crushed by girls, gritting my teeth as I listened to her get showered in compliments. As she flipped her silver hair with a *whoosh*, she replied, "Heh-heh-heh. I mean, this *is* me we're talking about! Duh!"

As for me…

"Ard! M-my name is Crea!"

"Hey, don't try to worm your way in! You can just ignore her, Ard!"

"Please go out with me and keep marriage in miiiiiiiiiiiiiind!"

"Damn! She beat me to it!"

"…Ha-ha."

This was certainly something that had never happened before. Meaning I was completely lost.

The last time I was in school, none of this would have ever happened, since the other students ostracized me as "that thing in the corner" or "Mister Invisible" and laughed at me behind my back. How did that turn into this? It was like I'd become the protagonist in one of those cliché young-adult romance novels.

…All thanks to my status, I bet.

You see, I was a nobody the last time I was a student. But now, I was a son of the Great Mages, which was exactly the reason why people followed my every move. Yeah, that had to be it. And it made me happy, seeing as I wasn't on the receiving end of fearful or dismissive looks for once. They were treating me like one of them, which was a really big deal—that said, I did have one hang-up.

"Tch. Those commoners better pipe down."

"Wish they'd just die. Damn! They're all annoying as shit."

As I took notice of a smaller crowd whispering among themselves from the distance, I realized my school life wasn't gonna be all fun and games. And I knew exactly who was to blame: the headmaster. That guy provoked the hell out of my new class, and the boys in particular couldn't stand me.

How am I gonna respond to the abuse coming my way? I felt sharp pangs in my gut as I mulled it over. I hadn't felt this bad since an army of gods drove me into a corner…!

Just as I was very seriously weighing my future actions, I heard another voice.

"…Dis…ing."

"St…"

As the other students chatted among themselves, I picked out the sounds of a particularly disagreeable conversation—a random boy hurling insults at someone else. I cast my eyes in their direction and spotted a boy with cropped orange hair slicked all the way back with far-set bug eyes and the boyish face of a reptile. And there was also…a girl with peach-colored hair.

Based on their uniforms, I could tell they were the rich kids. That boy was an elf, no doubt. Well, his facial features were all scrunched up in a rage, which wasn't very elven of him, but his pointed ears matched those of Ireena.

As for the girl... Well, she didn't have any discerning physical features, but I could feel a mysterious power radiating off her. Her peach-pink hair came down to her shoulders, framing skin the color of porcelain. A mature beauty. A peek at her low-cut uniform revealed shapely breasts and voluptuous thighs. Her body...sparked a flame of desire within me. Involuntarily.

Hmm. I bet this chick was a succubus, an especially rare race.

Anyway, the elven brat was dumping abuse on her.

"Color me surprised. Never would have thought a stupid hack would get accepted by the academy. What, did ya bribe the head-master with your body?" he sneered maniacally.

"N-no, I would never..." She sniffled in response.

It was a revolting scene to say the least.

"...I'm sorry, are you acquainted with those two?" I asked the crowd around me.

"Huh? Y-yeah. The boy's Elrado. He's kind of a big deal. From the House of Duke Burks, and a child prodigy at that. And the other girl is...Ginny. She's famous for having no talent whatsoever, even though she's from an incredibly renowned duchy."

"Her family serves his...and it seems he's always bullied her."

"Huh. Well... I'm afraid that just won't do." I glared at them.

If I made a move now, I would stick out in the worst possible way. But what of it? I was already destined to be bullied at this academy, so I had nothing to lose.

I got ready to raise my voice in protest.

"You there, stop this instant! Can't you see she doesn't like it?!" Ireena's voice rang out angrily before mine.

...Yeah, this was why we were friends.

When Elrado locked his eyes on his new target, I stepped forward. "She's right. You ought to apologize to Ginny."

In response, Elrado clicked his tongue before answering with "The airheaded daughter of the Heroic Baron and the idiotic son of the Great Mages. Well, well, well. I guess Mommy and Daddy got it in your heads that you're some special snowflakes, huh?"

"That's beside the point. Apologize to Ginny this instant and promise never to torment her ag—"

"Shaddup, dumb-ass." Elrado spat at my feet, sending the students into an uproar.

"Yeah, you show 'em, Elrado!"

"How could he disgrace the son of the Great Mages…? Do prodigies fear nothing?"

I ignored their cries. "I'm guessing you won't consider our request."

"Hmm. If you win against me in a duel, I guess I might? Assuming you're not a coward."

In any normal circumstance, Ireena would have barked back at him…but she glared at Elrado in frustration and unexpectedly left it at that.

"What's wrong, Ireena? I thought you'd be quick to accept his challenge."

"I…can't go up against that kid. At least, not without caution. He's been called the greatest genius of the century and a child of the gods… I mean, he's in the fourth rank of mages, or a Square, even though we're the same age…"

Oh, I see. This guy was powerful enough that even Ireena feared losing to him.

Just as I was thinking, *All right, then I'll—*

"Hey. What's going on?" demanded a woman's voice, causing everyone to tense up as it echoed throughout the classroom.

Someone was standing in the doorway—a therianthrope. The cat ears on her head were coupled with jet-black hair that reached down to her waist, and a tail sprouted from her rear. Her skin was a translucent lily white. She was about the same height as me, which put her on the tall side for a woman. Whether it was on purpose or not, her dismissively cold looks entranced others around her. And her clothing seemed to prioritize function over form, seeing as they were…pretty revealing for ease of movement and boldly exposed her soft thighs.

…No, wait. One sec. Wh-why was *she* here? Unless she had a doppelgänger, this woman was—

"L-Lady Olivia?!"

"What?! Y-you mean the legendary apostle…?!"

"I'd heard she was teaching as a special instructor at the academy…but to bask in her countenance on the very first day…!"

Th-that's right. She was one of the Four Heavenly Kings—my top commander and right-hand woman, Olivia vel Vine…!

W-w-wait. Hold on. Why is she here of all places? I mean, based solely on the fact that she was one of the Four Heavenly Kings, I was absolutely certain that she would have been out there ruling some nation or other—

"Tch. Day one and the class I'm in charge of is already picking fights, huh. Damn, what a pain."

Wh-what was that…?! Th-this was bad—r-r-real bad.

Oh god, I bet she'd be super pissed to find out that I reincarnated. She'd never, ever forgive me for acting all irresponsible and abandoning my kingly duties. If she found out about my true form… Oh, I—I don't even want to think about it. And now she's going to be my homeroom teacher? Gimme a break. At this rate, the risk of getting caught is, like, exponentially higher… I mean, first of all…

"…Is this mess your doing? Son of the Great Mages?"

First of all, I'd already managed to make a bad impression. She totally had her eye on me. B-but everything was still okay. I mean, there was no way she would realize my true form just yet. All I had to do was continue playing the role of Ard Meteor to a T.

"L-Lady Olivia. You're in good spirits, as usual…"

"'As usual'? I believe this is the first time we've met."

D-dammit! I totally panicked and chatted her up like an old friend!

"...Hmph. Well, whatever. Explain to me what happened here." Olivia's cat ears twitched.

I timidly informed her of the situation.

"Fine, I'll allow the duel. Hurry and get it over with before first period starts."

"N-no, I'm not saying I accepted—"

"Damn, you're a fussy one. Shut up and wrap it up. Show me what you've got." Olivia's tail swished back and forth as she spoke.

The class fell into an uproar all over again.

"H-hey, what was that just now...?!"

"O-Olivia wants to see his potential...!"

"Amazing! It's no surprise that he'd grab her attention! He's the son of the Great Mages, after all!"

Everyone was looking on with such envy, but...

You guys have no idea.

She was looking at me with marked suspicion, that was for sure. She always glared when she was onto someone, with her tail and ears twitching like crazy. If I wasn't on my best behavior during this duel, there was a good chance she'd piece together that Ard was the Demon Lord.

And to be honest, this was an even bigger problem than some battle against "the child of the gods" or whatever.

CHAPTER 5
The Ex–Demon Lord Versus the Child of the Gods

I made my way over, stomach churning in dread...as I reached the field where I was set to square off with Elrado. From a distance, Olivia, Ireena, and my other classmates watched over us.

"Whoa, whoa, whoa."

"That dude's as good as dead."

"Elrado is the youngest guy in history to make it to the fourth rank and receive the title of a Square. And a child prodigy at that."

"It wouldn't surprise me if he blew past the Great Mages and Heroic Baron."

As the spectators chattered among themselves, the aristocrats shot me a look of pointed pity, and Elrado gave me a vicious snarl—I mean, smile. Either way, it made his reptilian features seem five times more fiendish than usual.

"You've got some lousy luck, Snowflake. If Lady Olivia hadn't been there, you would have gotten outta this scot-free," he scoffed, eyeing me as if I'd volunteered to be a human sacrifice. His eyes held nothing but pure condescension.

Well, I guess I should have expected him to treat me this way. After all, this kid was a genius known as the "child of the gods," and

I, the most average villager in the world. But…something was off about this whole thing—to be precise, he really didn't seem impressive enough to be called "child of the gods" or whatever. At any rate, I had to observe my opponent to evaluate his skills.

"Well, let's get this over with—die already," Elrado barked, thrusting out his right palm.

A magic circle materialized directly in front of his eyes, spitting out a succession of small bolts: *Lightning Shot*, an elementary attack spell. He talked big, but it seemed he wanted to test me before making any major moves.

This spell wasn't a big deal at all. I cast *Wall*, a measly elementary spell of my own, calling forth a magic circle to allow a translucent barrier to envelop my immediate surroundings and cancel out his *Lightning Shot*.

This kind of barrage was nothing new to me.

"I—I can't believe Elrado cast *Lightning Burst* without an incantation…!"

"But Ard's keeping pace with him! I mean, he just cast *Mega Wall*! With no incantation!"

"Geez, if that were me, I'd be smashed to smithereens…! They're honestly out of this world…!"

Huh? Hold up. What's with this reaction? Don't tell me they're shocked that I didn't need to chant anything. Oh, and Lightning Burst? Mega Wall? Why was everyone mistaking our spells for mid-level ones?

"Ha! Cool, cool. You've got some fight in you after all, even though you're the idiot son of the Great Mages. Eh, fine. I take back that 'snowflake' comment from earlier."

"…Um, was there something in that little back-and-forth that made you want to rethink things?"

"Hmph. Don't get too comfortable. If you thought I've already shown you my best, you're dead wrong."

"That's what I figured. For you, that couldn't have been more than a warm-up."

"...You better watch your damn mouth!"

Whoa. Why was he getting all angry at me? I didn't say anything wrong. I mean, this level of magic should be nothing for a child of the gods.

Elrado's face contorted in rage as he unleashed his second attack—*Flare*, another elementary attack spell... Geez, he talked all tough, but he was *still* trying to size me up. I obstructed his efforts with *Wall*.

"Huh. I'm surprised you're still standing after having a taste of my *Mega Flare*."

"What? *Mega Flare*?"

...Seriously, what was this dude talking about? He had to know *Mega Flare* was mid-level, right? I mean, the spell had the word *Mega* in it for a reason. It was in a totally different league from your average *Flare*...which meant he must have been duping others into thinking his attacks were more advanced. A son from a noble family, my ass. Yeah, that had to be it. There was no other probable explanation.

"Heh. I'm gettin' pretty pumped. It's been a while since I could go all out...!"

"...This is only making you look more ridiculous, you know."

"*Huh?* What're you blabbin' on about, dumb-ass?"

"I'm just saying I've unmasked your true nature. This whole 'child of the gods' business is a sham—all to pad your overinflated ego. I bet you begged your parents to falsify and spread those rumors."

"...*What?*"

Bull's-eye. A vein popped on Elrado's temple.

"Now, now. Calm down. I can understand where you're coming from. I've been through that phase, too, you know. Like calling some low-level spells by embarrassing names—even when they have legitimate ones. As boys, we all have a phase when we want to seem stronger. But wow. To call yourself a child of the gods. That's overkill. Plus, you don't even live up to the name. In terms of wit, you're a child of the most average pare—"

"*You're goin' dooooooown!*" Elrado snapped, which meant I was right on the money.

Goodness, I was stupid for thinking I needed to be cautious.

"Congrats, bastard! You're the first one to piss me off this much!"

"Is that so? Well, same goes for me. I've never met a dunce who contradicts his own unmerited title. First time for everything, I guess."

"*Damn youuuuuuuu!*" Elrado boomed, scrunching his face into a demonic glare as he invoked his magic.

From my perspective, it was horseplay at best—a cheap, pointless diversion. In an instant, I was surrounded by his magic circles that had appeared in every direction. He was planning to fire off multiple *Flares* at once. How unimpressive. I mean, he was treating me like a kid, unleashing this spell as if it was his deadly finishing move.

Anyway, I put up another *Wall* as the flames threatened to close in on me and neutralized his attacks with a copper-colored film that covered my body from head to toe. No biggie. At least for me.

"Wha…?! H-how…?!"

"H-he fended off a special spell from the House of Duke Burks! A *Giga Flare*?!"

Huh? A Giga Flare? *You callin' that a* Giga Flare?

"Don't tell me my *Giga Flare* was useless…?! Y-yeah, right!"

Erm, I hate to break it to you, but you unleashed a bunch of regular Flares. *Don't go around referring to your measly attack with the name of a high-level spell…*

Plus, I was the creator of spells powered by ancient runes. I was sorely disappointed by his actions, that was for sure. It was honestly sinful to say this was anywhere near advanced.

"…Elrado. You've made a grave mistake."

"Huh?! What are you—?"

"It seems you don't know the real deal. Allow me to show you a true *Giga Flare*," I declared, visualizing a magic circle in my mind's eye.

As it swelled with energy, a ten-merel circle appeared beneath his feet, releasing a gale of flames that tore through the earth.

"Whoaaaaaa?!"

"Wh-what is this magic?! I can feel the heat from back here!"

"Eeeeeeeeeek!"

A roaring, swirling crimson hellfire: Now, *this* was *Giga Flare*. Its attack range was small and concentrated, making it one of the strongest single-target combat spells.

Elrado had managed to cast *Wall* beforehand—not that it'd do him much good. *Giga Flare* would tear through his defenses without leaving behind a single piece of ash, meaning I had no choice but to cast a mid-level defense spell for him. All five layers of it, and while maintaining control of *Giga Flare*. But even that wasn't enough to withstand its heat.

As the invocation finally burned through its magical energy, the effect of the spell tapered off, revealing Elrado's charred body. It crumpled onto the ground.

"Wh-whoa... I-is he dead...?"

"Duh. He underestimated the son of the Great Mages."

"He got what he deserved."

Wrong. Elrado wasn't dead. I made sure he wouldn't die. I wouldn't want to pointlessly take a life; that wasn't my style. And on top of that, it'd be more trouble than it was worth for a commoner (me) to kill a noble heir.

...In either case, why was everyone and their cousin practically jumping out of their skin? I mean, sure, he was a bit scratched up, but anyone could fix him, easy.

When I cast *Heal*, another one of those elementary spells, his entire body became covered in a large magic circle.

"Ah...?! D-did I die just now...?!"

It'd be more accurate to say you almost died, buddy.

With eyes like saucers, Elrado continued to mutter incoherently to himself—buck naked. Well, it wasn't that I *couldn't* give him back his clothes, but I honestly couldn't be bothered.

"""*D-did he come back to life?!*""" a chorus of voices cried out.

Geez, I've been trying to tell you that he was never dead to begin with.

For starters, even if I had brought him back from the dead, it wouldn't have been a particularly impressive feat, especially while his human spirit was still loitering around in this world—basically, anytime for three days after death. As long as you took the proper measures before then, anyone could be brought back to life, no problem. I was honestly more surprised that this wasn't common knowledge for students attending such a prestigious school.

Anyway, I approached Elrado, looking down on him.

"I hope you understand. What you witnessed just now was a true *Giga Flare*. Please make sure you don't commit the same mistake going forward," I warned slowly to drive that point home, emanating a menacing aura of *I won't forgive you next time.*

Elrado nodded emphatically. Where was his senselessly high self-esteem? Seriously? Did a single brush with death break his spirit? How pathetic.

"Well then, Elrado. I'm sure we can agree that I'm the winner of this duel, right?"

He continued to nod with increased vigor.

Whoa. I can almost see an afterimage trailing behind his bobbing head.

"Very well. I'd like you to keep your promise now and apologize to Ginny—"

"*I'm so sorry for everything, Lady Ginny! I will never harm you*

*again! You will never see me before you again! Please! Please for-
give me!"* Elrado skidded onto the ground, groveling marvelously
before her.

Huh. To think one near-death experience was all it took to turn
him around. I bet he wasn't such a bad guy after all.

But I seriously doubted we'd ever be friends, unfortunately,
seeing as he was eyeing me in the exact same way as my former subordinates and the general public had ogled me...in other words, in
all-consuming fear. I knew better than to try to form a friendship
with anyone who looked at me that way. It broke my heart, to be
honest.

I heaved a heavy sigh just as Olivia approached me. "Hey, you. The
son of our great heroes."

I was unwittingly startled by her cool tone. "Y-yes, Lady Olivia?
Everything I did was totally average—"

"You invoked your spell and cast another one over Elrado at the
same time, right?"

"Y-yes. Is there something wrong?"

"In other words, you did a *Double Cast*."

"Wh-what about it?"

"A *D-Double Cast*?! Y-you're kidding?!"

"E-even the son of the Great Mages couldn't possibly...!"

Th-this reaction again?

"U-um. Just a simple *Double Cast*. Yep. I'd be surprised to see someone cast twenty or thirty spells at a time, sure, but I don't see why a—"

"In this era, that 'simple *Double Cast*' is considered a *Lost Skill*."

"...I'm sorry?"

A *L-Lost Skill*? A *Double Cast*? Really?

I didn't understand. I couldn't help but break into a cold sweat
just as Olivia grabbed both my shoulders firmly and snorted.

...Oh, this was bad. This was *really* bad.

"So this is the child of the Great Mages, huh? All your spells are considered *Lost Skills*. You've done a splendid job of demonstrating them to us."

"B-but doesn't something become a *Lost Skill* only when it doesn't get handed down and dies out? Um, like *Ultimatum Zero*, for example."

I brought up the case of a special attack spell that only the Demon Lord (me) had been able to cast. That'd be a *Lost Skill* for sure, but this? No chance.

"Well, after the Demon Lord died, there was a huge shift in mana in the atmosphere, you see. It diluted considerably. I'm guessing you know what *mana* means, don't you? The source of magical energy in all living beings. This means spells are far weaker today than in the past—because of the rapid decline in the amount of mana."

"I-is that so?"

"Yeah. But you think your spells are perfectly normal." Olivia gave me a menacing smile.

"Your sense of 'normal' aligns with ancient values. Your way of thinking couldn't be further from the norm in today's magically degenerative world. Your *Giga Flare*? That's known as *Ultima Flare* in this day and age. It's undoubtedly one of the most famous among the *Lost Skills*. And it's known as a superspecial attack spell.

"Plus, your *Double Cast* is another one of those unattainable techniques. That's right, even your parents—the Great Mages—can't cast two spells at once." Olivia paused, her black ears and tail twitching, as she let out the slightest of smiles. "I wonder: Why in the world would you think your ancient standards are the norm?"

     ....

     ....

...Ah, I see. That explains it.

That was why everyone was showering me with praise, even though I was some random villager. Sure, I'd reincarnated as an average human, thanks to my spell. But that's where the problem had started: I'd become an "average human" according to my standards... But in this modern, magically deteriorated society, I was still extraordinary.

Ha-ha-ha. I'm screwed—so, so screwed.

Ha-ha-ha-ha-ha-ha. Ha-ha-ha-ha-ha-ha-ha-ha-ha-ha-ha.

....

....*Someone help me.*

"Well, ain't it strange? I feel so nostalgic when I'm near your magical energy. Weird, right?" Olivia's grip on my shoulders was tightening by the second, pressing my heels harder into the ground.

At the same time, my stomach was twisting and turning in new directions as she beamed at me.

"Hey, Ard Meteor... What are you?"

CHAPTER 6
The Ex–Demon Lord in High-Key Danger

Even in a million years, I never would have imagined that the death of the Demon Lord would cause a magical revolution, much less dilute airborne mana, which led us...here.

"I'll ask once more, Ard Meteor. What in the world are you?" And my ex-right-hand woman was trying to murder me.

"Oh, Lady Olivia is smiling...!"

"Even though she's famous for being expressionless...!"

"I'd expect no less from the son of the Great Mages! I mean, we've hardly finished the entrance ceremony, and he's already caught her eye!"

Wrong again. She doesn't make this expression when she takes a liking to someone. This is her "Should I kill this guy? Hmm, what to do?" face.

You see, when Olivia was in a sour mood, she became a peppy little chatterbox. On the other hand, when she was happy, she'd zip her mouth tighter than usual and play childish pranks on you. Oh, and it was completely possible to guess her thoughts at any given time by observing her cat ears and tail.

As of right now...she absolutely suspected me of being the Demon

Lord Varvatos. No, more than suspected. Wait… Had she already made up her mind?

"Son of the Great Mages. Do you have anything you want to say?"

Ha-ha, that's not it. Right, Olivia? You're not actually trying to ask me that. You mean: Do you have any last words? *I'm guessing you're gonna kill me now, right? Right?*

…I've got to know why things turned out this way. Question the party responsible for all this. Someone, anyone—please call them.

…Ah, so this was the end. I'd at least fight until I was completely done for.

As cold sweat poured down from every part of my body, I locked eyes with Olivia.

"I'm the son of the Great Mages. Nothing more, nothing less."

We continued to stare each other down.

"Fair enough. I suppose I'm satisfied. For now."

Was I safe for the time being…?! I heaved out a huge sigh of relief as Olivia pivoted and sauntered away.

This woman was known as "Olivia," my right-hand woman who I could trust more than anyone else… To me, she'd acted the part of an older sister, and I was sure she'd loved me as a younger brother at one time.

That was to say, until I became the Demon Lord.

I couldn't place my finger on the exact moment it'd happened, but I realized as time passed that she'd ended up in the position of my underling, putting up invisible boundaries between us. That's when I realized that I'd been locked up…in a prison cell of loneliness. I guess I'd been operating on false pretenses that she alone would always be on equal footing with me—which was exactly why her betrayal tormented me the most… In truth, I'd partly reincarnated into this new body to spite her.

Oh, and to clear up one thing: This wasn't my fault. Honestly, 80 percent of the blame was on Olivia.

...Well, even if that was the absolute truth, this present situation wasn't going to change anytime soon.

I mean, if she found out my past identity, she'd throttle me—even though I didn't do anything wrong. Best-case scenario, she'd beat the living crap out of me. Worst case? I could say bye-bye to my social life. If I could have hightailed it out of here, I would've in an instant. But I had to preserve my parents' dignity—plus, it'd only confirm her suspicions that I'm actually the Demon Lord.

I'm guessing she still wasn't absolutely sure about my true self. Which meant the best plan would be to quietly go about as a normal student at the academy. That'd clear away her suspicions for sure.

That settles it. I made my way over to my very first class.

The clock ticked dangerously close to our starting time when our teacher strolled into our class. It was Jessica, whose silky platinum locks swayed behind her as she walked into the room. Upon surveying the class and confirming that I was there with Ireena, she broke out into a bewitching grin.

"Hee-hee-hee. We meet again," she cooed.

This caused a bit of a stir among the students.

"I didn't realize they had connections with *this* genius...and a marquis at that...!"

"I'm thinking we ought to get buddy-buddy with them. They'll come in handy when we need to network someday."

The commoners displayed their honest surprise, while the aristocrats plotted some more of their wicked little schemes. Jessica finally reached the podium, casting a glance in our general direction before aiming a pointed stare toward the front corner by the entrance.

"Oh, and by the way...why is the legendary apostle here? One instructor per class is plenty," Jessica observed.

She was talking about Olivia, who'd been in the classroom this whole time, standing unflinching in the corner to glare at me.

"…There's a student who caught my eye. I won't be a disturbance. Think of me as air," Olivia suggested.

The class began to rumble again.

"That's gotta be him."

"Wow, of course. Ard's gotten ahold of Lady Olivia's heart…!"

"Oh, gosh. If she's my rival for his love, this battle's already been decided…"

Wrong, and wrong again. It went without saying that our relationship wasn't in any way romantic.

"Huh, that so? Well, in that case, go ahead," Jessica answered casually before turning to address the rest of the class.

"Well, then. Welcome to the study of magical transmutation. For the first half of our lesson, we'll be going over the history of magic potions. After that, I'll score you with a practical exam on transmutations. You need fifty percent or more to pass, and anyone who fails will be pounded with supplementary lessons—without mercy. Prepare yourselves," Jessica announced, planting her hands on her hips and sticking out her chest with a big old grin.

I guess the majority of the students in the class, especially the boys, perceived this pose of hers as adorable and charming. There were quite a few who appeared absolutely transfixed by her.

Jessica pinched a piece of chalk between her slim fingers and began writing all across the blackboard with an elegant flick of her wrist.

"As many of you know, the use of potions is still relatively new. Its first recorded case was close to five hundred years ago. One of the Four Heavenly Kings, Sir Verda the Apostle, stumbled across potions when he was trying to find a substitute for healing spells, which were undergoing a rapid decline. Using the medicines he'd developed, he created a prototype for…" Jessica droned on.

The lecture continued. No problems so far. Jessica's sonorous voice echoed throughout the silent classroom, accompanied by the crescendo of scratches as the chalk hit against the blackboard.

"Which means potions have done us a lot of good—as a substitute for healing spells. Let's see…for example, think back on the incident that's better left unsaid. Yes, ten years back, the Evil God was resurrected by the demons, leading to civilian causalities. Without enough healers on hand, we resorted to using potions and—"

No sooner had *demons* and *Evil God* left Jessica's mouth than the atmosphere in the room totally shifted. Before, all the students had been unruffled and attentive…until those taboo words sent everyone into a nervous panic.

Well, that was reasonable, seeing as how their religion put the Demon Lord on a pedestal, meaning any of his enemies were fair game to hate on. On top of that, the demons were still well and alive, terrorizing modern civilization and striking fear into their hearts. That was plenty enough to justify this hostility.

In the middle of all this, Ireena was the only one hanging her head sadly. Just as I was asking myself why, Jessica interrupted me.

"All righty. That's enough lecturing for now, so let's move on to the practical exam."

Another woman assisted in hustling ingredients for potion transmutations into the classroom, along with some kind of sorcery device. Jessica plucked out a box about the size of her palm.

"This right here will measure the effectiveness of your potions. You'll all take turns pouring your final product into this tube, and then it'll display a number based on its potency. I'll be grading you on that score. Just make sure you get higher than fifty percent!"

With that, we trucked the materials to our desks and got to work.

"Hey, Ard. Let's have a contest to see who can get the higher score!" Ireena suggested.

"I wouldn't mind."

"Heh-heh-heh. I won't lose this time!" she declared, jabbing a finger in my direction with a triumphant smile.

How charming. She cleanses my soul—from all the stress brought on by that damn Olivia.

But I wasn't about to put up a fair fight, unfortunately. I'd already decided to let her win, because I was planning to make the most average, most regular potion of all time.

And with that, I promptly started to work. We were assigned to make a potion to treat wounds using three blades of Nelgi Grass, two pieces from the root of a Mitsumi plant, and two wings from a Morgan Butterfly. Using a mortar and pestle, I ground the dry ingredients down into a fine powder before dissolving it into some water in a vessel.

After that, I used hydro-alchemy to transcribe a special-class magic circle onto the desk. I placed the vessel on top and supplied it with magic.

Even though the use of potions hadn't been explored yet in my past life, I'd familiarized myself with how to mix and create potions by poring over textbooks in our home library during my childhood.

That said, I was surprised that they used these special magic circles for a procedure as simple as potion making. I mean, back in the good old days, we'd reserved them for major ceremonies or to cast spells that required the magical energy of more than one person. I guess the state of magic in this world was worse than I'd previously thought.

Anyway, I pushed all that thinking aside to make a potion according to the textbook at home.

Awesome. Totally mediocre.

And the same color as everyone else's potions to boot—a vibrant green. On the other hand, Ireena's concoction was bubbling crimson, unlike any other one in the class.

"Heh-heh-heh. How does it feel to lose?" she chided.

"Ha-ha-ha, we'll see. We won't know who won until we cross the finish line," I cautioned, but I was full-on ready to lose and see my darling little Ireena delightfully assume her victory pose. But that was beside the point.

By this time, everyone had finished concocting their potions.

Jessica nodded. "All righty, let's start with the front row. Get in line and come up to the podium, please."

The students began to move forward in unison.

"Hmm, this device is giving me three hundred points for your potion. Meaning you score thirty-five percent. I'll have you join me for some super-fun remedial lessons."

"Whaaaaaaaat?!" the boy lamented despite his expression of pure joy.

Jessica assigned more and more students to extra coursework, though none of the boys seemed particularly down about their results. Well, I guess it made sense in a way. With a curvy beauty for a teacher, anyone would jump at the opportunity to stick around for a few extra lessons.

At any rate, the line in front of us shrank until it was our row's turn. We clambered out of our seats and made our way through the class to the podium, where we began to receive our results one after the other. Ireena was up next. Honestly, she was the type of girl who made every guy want to give her half the world.

Ireena poured her potion into the device with pride etched all across her face, confident of her impending victory.

"Nice…!" Jessica's eyes almost popped out of her head. "One thousand two hundred points! Amazing job, Ireena! One hundred percent!"

Upon hearing this grand reveal, Ireena puffed out her chest adorably and cast a few inconspicuous looks in my direction.

"Heh-heh-heh! A piece of cake, really! *(glance)*" she boasted in a thinly veiled attempt to hide her usual attention-seeking.

That said, her face was totally plastered with *You know you can praise me, right? C'mon, please! Woof, woof!*

Oh geez. This smug little face of hers was way too cute to handle. Meaning, of course, that I happily obliged her request.

"Wonderful job. You're the best of the best, Ireena."

"Heh-heh-heh-heh. Well, what can I say? That's who I am!" she chirped, practically melting in my hands as I stroked her silver hair.

Her facial expression dissolved into a sloppy mess as she closed her eyes in complete and utter contentment. Kind of like a dog praised by its owner. This puppy side of Ireena was seriously too cute.

"...An honest young maiden. Unlike when Weiss was at the academy," noted Olivia in a low mutter.

Ireena's head snapped up. "What?! Did you know my daddy when he was younger?!"

"Y-yeah," Olivia stuttered, taking a step back in total bewilderment as Ireena pushed her way closer to her with sparkles in her eyes.

"Ooh, please tell me tales about his school days!"

"W-we're in the middle of class. If you really want, ask me in the staff room later," Olivia advised, to which Ireena bobbed her head eagerly.

Olivia looked completely at a loss as to how to handle this excitable ball of energy since it was rare for others to interact with her with such blinding innocence and naïveté. It'd been a while since I'd seen Olivia with an openly flustered expression.

Huh. I guess I forgot that she has a soft side—

"Hey, son of the Great Mages. Who do you think you're smirkin' at? I'll smack that grin right off your face."

Erm. I take that back. Yep. She inspires as much fear as ever. Just like an older sister.

After a few other students received their assessments, it was finally my turn.

"Up next, Ard… Hee-hee-hee, I'm expecting a lot from you, Mr. Child Genius," Jessica called out.

But she wasn't the only one anticipating my evaluation. Every single student in the class was eyeing my potion and me, looking all anxious. Even Olivia was glaring at me with a stern expression on her face.

Ha. Stare all you want. But mine is absolutely, totally, completely normal. No surprises here—

"W-wait, an error…?! *Immeasurable*…?!" Jessica yelped.

—Hold up.

"H-how can that be…?!" she stammered. "This device can even measure the strength of the most potent elixirs, but… N-no, wait… I-it can't be… Is this the Essence of Philosopher's Stone…?!"

Um, no, actually…

The classroom broke into a sea of panicked cries.

"Th-the Essence of Philosopher's Stone?!"

"The one from fairy tales…?!"

"You can't possibly mean the legendary potion, right? The one that gives those who drink it supernatural strength? Or raise them from the dead…?!"

Wait a sec. C'mon. Please.

"U-um. Well, this is, er, a regular potion, isn't it?" I clarified. "I mean, the Essence of Philosopher's Stone isn't even in the same league. And I followed the instructions on my parents' book exactly, so I can assure you that this is nothing but a normal potion."

"…And the title of the book?"

U-um… What was it? Oh yeah, now I remember.

"I believe it was *The History of Altria-Style Transmutation*."

"*Th-The History of Altria-Style Transmutation*?! You mean the ultrarare book by the legendary transmutationist Master Altria?!"

"*Whaaaaaaaaaaaat*?!" I gaped.

Th-that stupid book?! Ultrarare? No way! …Awww, crap! I forgot!

My parents are the Great Mages! Of course they don't have any old library! I screwed up big-time!

"...The Essence of Philosopher's Stone? It seems like quite the creation, eh?" Olivia commented.

D-dammit! Her whole face is getting brighter! She's actually smiling for crying out loud!

"N-no! Th-this is, well..." I tried to deflect. "Oh yeah! It's all thanks to my mother and father! Yep. All thanks to their possession of this legendary book. Without it, I would have never—"

"Sure. In fact, the transmutation of potions depends entirely on creating the magic circle that corresponds to the technique."

"Yep! That's right! That's what I'm saying! Which all means it wasn't a big—"

"Now, hold on. In order to properly transmute this, you would need enough magical energy to activate the magic circle. To fulfill the needs of this one, you'd require tens of thousands of times more than your average spell...! If you're able to supply this power all on your own, we've got no choice but to call this a big deal!"

DAMMIT, STOP MAKING THINGS WOOOOOORSE!

"T-tens of thousands?"

"He's in a different dimension compared to the rest of us..."

"Heh-heh-heh! Are you impressed yet?! That's Ard for ya! And he's *my* friend!" Ireena sang out, standing proud and tall. I could almost hear her thinking, *Whaddaya think? Isn't he the best?*

She was looking as sweet as always, but to be honest, it was only making matters more out of control.

"She's right. He's amazing. That's for sure," Olivia agreed.

Aghhhhh... She's looking so gleeeeeeeeeful... She's practically beeeeeeeeeaming...

"Ha-ha-ha. Ard Meteor, huh. You're really somethin' else, aren't you?"

Eek?! I-is she laughiiiing?! Whyyyyy is she laughing?!

O-oh geez. We're at the part where she kills me, aren't we?!

"Hee-hee-hee. You've really grown on me, Ard."

AAAAAAAAAH! She called me by my name! My first name! No one's ever been called by their first name and lived to tell the tale! Foreshadowing my death, I see!

A—a—a plan! I've gotta think up a plan! And fast!

CHAPTER 7
The Ex–Demon Lord and His Plans to Support a New Student

I had frantically tried to clear Olivia's misgivings for some time…but all my efforts were in vain. Her smile had stretched across her face inch by inch, accompanied by a violent air around her, practically screaming, *This guy's the Demon Lord, right? Should I punish him? I think I should.*

And then, it was lunchtime, and following that, the last period of the day, held at the underground dungeon.

These spaces are enveloped in a dense mana that allows the core to generate and maintain a predetermined number of monsters at any given time. On one hand, these underground dungeons are fraught with danger—on the other, they're absolutely brimming with rare monster parts. Those who raid them to earn money and perform this public service are called "Dungeon Seekers."

Because our academy touted a policy of educating well-rounded students, we had to learn a myriad of subjects that weren't exactly relevant to magic, unlike some other schools. As a result, our alum branched out into innumerable career paths—including the notorious Dungeon Seekers.

I'd grown used to these spaces by now. Enclosed in stone from all sides, the dungeon was covered in a layer of moss emitting a faint glow, and the air was cool, instantly setting on edge whoever stepped foot inside. We stood at the entrance as our instructor's drawling voice echoed through the air.

"Everyone, just relaaaax, okay? The upper levels are noooooo biggie," he claimed in a slow voice that robbed anyone listening of all their worry.

His exterior was gentle and sweet, as expected of all halflings, but don't let that fool you. According to the grapevine, he'd once been a great adventurer.

…Unsurprisingly, Olivia stood off to the side, her ears and tail twitching as she smiled at me. Oh, the things I would do to snatch that grin right off her face.

"This is our very first lesson, so I think I'll make it niiiice and easy," he commented before motioning us to follow him so he could teach us how to hunt and take apart a monster.

"Well theeeen, time for your assiiiiiiignment. Go waaaay down to the third level and defeat a Black Wolf. Bring its hide to me, and I'll check its quality. Then I'll give you a score, got iiiiiiiit?" he practically yawned out…and then unleashed a serious blow to the heart. "All rightyyyy, let's make teams of three. For this assignment, you'll be working in a paaaaarty."

Needless to say, the word *team* is low-key forbidden when you're a loner. I refused to recount the memories associated with this word. *I mean, what is the point of reliving the past anyway? What matters is the present.*

"Ard! Please join my party!"

"Hey! I wanna work with him!"

There was no harm in enjoying a reality where my classmates actually wanted to be on my team. They descended on Ireena and me in droves as soon as the instructor finished giving his instructions.

As I wondered how to respond to this unfamiliar situation, I couldn't help but break out into a small smile—when a girl standing all by herself caught my eye.

It was the beautiful succubus Ginny, the one who'd been bullied by Elrado. As she fiddled with her shoulder-length peach-colored hair, she nervously glanced around her, which instantly took me back to my own days at school during my past life: No one had invited either of us to be on their team, and yet neither of us had had the courage to reach out. As a result, we'd both ended up by ourselves.

Her blue eyes started to well up with tears, appearing embarrassed by her situation, and I wasn't about to let that pass. I excused myself from the crowd, trying to take a step toward her.

"Hey, Ginny! Come and join our party!" Ireena demanded.

She'd managed to bound toward the succubus before me, calling out to Ginny in a voice full of stubborn determination and affection. Just like the other students, Ginny's eyes had become as wide as saucers from disbelief until she was able to work her trembling lips to string together a coherent sentence.

"M-me? Really…?" she asked hesitantly, clasping her hands in front of her voluptuous chest.

Ireena left her no room for doubt. "Of course! Ard's got no objections, either. Right?!"

I smiled ever so slightly. "None whatsoever, Ireena."

This confirmed it: My daughter was the best—kind and overflowing with love. I couldn't help but wonder what might have happened if I'd met her in my past life.

Well, no use thinking about that now. We welcomed Ginny into our party and began our search.

The inside of the maze was breezy, causing the girls to shiver lightly in their skimpy school uniforms, though it'd be wholly inaccurate to say these chills were due to temperature alone. There was a peculiar sort of gloom that lingered within the maze and awakened a primordial fear, forcing the body to tremble of its own volition.

Beside me, Ginny was practically crushing her big boobs against each other as she cradled herself in her own arms, her eyes darting around fearfully. Her soft, milky thighs were daringly exposed and seductively turned inward...which naturally sparked a carnal desire in me that made me want to ravish her—this was a succubus's trademark. That said, I'd obviously do no such thing.

On the other hand, my dear Ireena was jovially singing as she scampered along.

"Ard! *A* is for *Annihilating Evil*! ♪ *R* is for *Runs 'Em Straight Through*! ♪ *D* is for *Decimate the Enemy*! ♪" Ireena blared, plunging fearlessly ahead, swinging her arms around, and humming an odd little tune. Her generous chest jiggled every time she let her arms sway in time with her tone-deaf voice.

It seemed both of us were used to these eerie surroundings. After all, we'd routinely made our way through the dungeons back in our home village.

As we pushed forward, the monsters in question appeared before my party: Black Wolves. These dark beasts measured less than one merel from the withers, slinking forward in a pack of ten. Ginny was startled enough to let out a tiny shriek, collapsing onto her butt and quivering in fear.

I grinned at this sight. "It's all right, Ginny. We can take care of these monsters—easily."

I snapped my fingers, unleashing a host of geometric patterns that served as magic circles around the Black Wolves and unfurling a flurry of flames. They didn't even last three seconds before they were burned to a crisp.

YOU DEFEATED THE BLACK WOLVES! A transparent gray message box popped up before us.

You could say that the dungeons were a world of their own. It honestly felt that way sometimes, considering how they operated on a different set of rules and seemingly a whole other plane of existence. This message box was just another one of those dungeon-exclusive elements that toyed with the common preconceptions of reality. They cropped up at various points: Following the defeat of a monster or retrieving items from a chest were just a few examples. The reason for their existence was shrouded in mystery, but I couldn't really say that I cared either way, so I had no plans to find out in the foreseeable future.

"Y-you defeated a pack of Black Wolves in an instant...! A-Ard, you're incredible...!"

"Heh-heh-heh! If you're shocked now, just you wait. This is the boy who took down an Ancient Wolf when he was...wait for it... twelve years old!"

"Whaaaaat?! An Ancient Wolf at twelve years old?!"

As I listened in on their conversation, I took a good look at the remains of the monsters in front of us and folded my arms. I had gone way overboard. There was nothing but ashes left. We wouldn't be able to bring back any of their hides at this rate. It was honestly really hard to go easy on anything.

"I-I'm honored to be in a party with you two. You're amazing, really. B-but...are you sure you want me on your team? ...I mean, all I'll do is drag you down...," Ginny whispered.

Hmph. It seemed this girl had a tendency to needlessly put herself down, though I could identify the culprit. She'd probably developed the habit from suffering under Elrado's torment since childhood.

I could relate. After all, I'd endured abuse during the

formative years in my past life, thousands of years ago. Like being called "girlie boy" for my feminine features and getting garbage chucked at me day after day. Or like the time I lost my family and home, when some people totally trashed my makeshift bed on the streets. I still can remember how they jeered, "*You ain't got no place to sleep*"...and all these experiences from a young age culminated in an inferiority complex. I was saved by my childhood friend, Olivia, but it didn't seem like Ginny had found her own savior—yet.

"Ginny, if you'd like, I could instruct you on the ways of magic. How about it?"

"What? Y-you mean you'll teach me?"

"Precisely. I'm inexperienced, but I hope my knowledge is enough to grant you the tiniest bit of confidence."

With power comes confidence, to a greater or lesser degree. I figured I'd toughen her up and give her some much-needed self-esteem.

"...I'll never be strong. That's for sure." Her eyes were cast downward, hidden by her bangs. But I could tell they were swimming with servility and anguish.

"No. You *can* be strong. I'll make sure of it. I swear," I declared as forcefully as possible.

Ginny raised her head timidly and glanced at me. "Wh-why? And why me...? I... Compared to you, I'm a tiny pebble at the edge of the road, right...?"

"Listen up, Ginny. In this world, there is no such thing. Each of us is a main character, living life to the fullest, and that includes you. You just don't know how to shine yet... I mean, you do want to succeed, don't you?"

"...That sounds just like...a line from a heroic ballad..." Ginny looked down again and mumbled incoherently.

Just as I started to worry that maybe it was a no-go, she snapped her head up with a *whoosh*.

"I-I'd love to!"

In her eyes, I saw a fighting spirit ready to say good-bye to the past.

And thus, I decided to educate the sad and lovely succubus.

CHAPTER 8
The Ex–Demon Lord's Lessons on Magic, Part I

I tried my very best to boost Ginny's strength by imparting some of my knowledge on her, attempting to teach her how to cast spells without using incantations, but all my efforts fell flat without a single notable success.

"...I knew it. I really am good for nothing," Ginny muttered, totally dejected.

I racked my brain, folding my arms as I thought through the best course of action: If I tried to console her now by assuring her of her true potential, it'd probably make her feel all the more pitiful—even if it was the *truth*. Plus, she wouldn't believe me. Not now. Not yet.

Even though Ginny was super self-deprecating, she couldn't be as worthless as she made it seem. I mean, no succubus could ever be considered incompetent. In fact, they were rare, even back in my day, with a bunch of them possessing incredible magical talent. Meaning Ginny was probably highly skilled in the magic arts herself.

It also meant that her mental state was the only possible reason for our lack of progress, since the efficiency and acquisition of magic fluctuated in accordance with it. Everything could change with the right amount of confidence and relaxation. The reverse was true as well: Your nerves could get in the way and prevent any power from manifesting.

...Truth be told, I didn't want to reveal my true magical capacity to anyone, but this was for the sake of Ginny's confidence. I just had to do it.

I let out a labored sigh. "You can't give up. I still have more to teach. For example... Oh, I guess there's one technique that I haven't even taught you, Ireena."

Ireena's eyes shone with curiosity, Ginny's with hope, as I got ready to begin my newest lecture.

"Perfect timing. Take this Black Wolf, for example," I declared, staring fixedly at the mangy mutt approaching us and swiping my finger in front of me—causing the area surrounding the beast to detonate.

And no overkill this time, either. Nice. The hide was perfectly serviceable while the wolf itself was dead as a log.

"...Huh? Wait, um... What?"

"A-Ard, wh-what did you do just now?"

The two stared at me in shock.

I answered them with a raised finger. "By using broken fragments of ancient runes, I first projected a simple magic circle in the air and cast a spell real quick. I call it 'Script Magic.'"

"'S-Script Magic'...?!"

"B-but I've never heard of such a thing...?!"

"I'm not surprised. I mean, I made it myself, after all."

"'Whaaaaaaaaa—?!'" the two girls shrieked.

"A-are you telling me you created your own method of casting spells?! Y-you do realize that pretty much makes you comparable with the Demon Lord, right?!" yelped Ginny.

"H-heh-heh-heh! Th-that's Ard for ya! Bask in his glory!" Ireena stuttered.

How unusual. For once, Ireena seemed rattled, even though I thought she'd grown used to my shenanigans.

...That's why I didn't want to show this off. I knew it wasn't normal, which meant trouble would follow its grand reveal. But I was desperate to make Ginny believe in herself, lift her out of the hell she'd found herself in—and save her the same way Olivia had saved me.

"W-wow, Ard... You've gotta be superspecial... I mean, I can't imagine anyone less talented than you would be able to use this kind of—"

"Wrong. Anyone is capable of casting this spell. I mean, I created it with that explicitly in mind."

"Come again?"

"Think about it: This spell draws on the powers of elementary magic circles formed from runes. Meaning you, and everyone else in this world, can cast it. All you need to do is draw a magic circle."

"W-wow... But I imagine you need a boatload of magical power to—"

"Not really. It's pretty close to nothing, you know."

""*Whaaaaaaaat?*"" they screeched—and totally in sync, to boot.

"N-no magical power necessary...?!"

"H-how is that possible?"

"Easy. The theory is laughably simple: The fragmentary runes draw on the mana in the air as an energy source in place of magic— which means, its powers activate the moment you project a magic circle," I explained, but I was still met with some skepticism.

My next move was to teach them more in-depth about the techniques associated with the rune language until Ireena was able to take down a wolf of her own.

YOU OBTAINED THE FUR OF A BLACK WOLF (NORMAL)! VALUE: 50, proclaimed the message box.

Ireena cocked her head quizzically. "Huh. I've noticed this before, but if this one's described as (NORMAL), I wonder if there's an (AMAZING) one, too."

Well, I can't say for sure, but I do know that you're (CUTE), I thought to myself as we trudged through the dungeon, managing to stumble upon another pack of wolves.

"This is perfect. Are you ready, Ginny?"

"Y-yes!" She gave a quick nod and began swiping her finger through the air—engulfing the pack in a gigantic explosion and leaving it totally obliterated.

"I—I did it…! I did it! I really did it! I cast the spell, Ard!" Ginny blurted out, radiating pure joy and bouncing up and down in uncontainable excitement.

Each time she hopped, her peach hair fluttered around her face and shoulders. And each time, her massive boobs wobbled, as well.

Ahem. *Anyway.*

Everything went according to plan, and Ginny had finally begun to sprout some much-needed confidence.

"I can't believe I don't need any magical power to cast this spell," she ruminated. "Think of what would happen if this ever went public. Our current hierarchy would be turned on its head…!"

"Ha-ha. Impossible. I mean, it could happen in theory. Like, a mage would be able to fight for an astronomically long time by relying on Script Magic, since their powers would never deplete. But because this method draws energy from mana, their attack spells would be small at best—which means it can't be used for more than keeping your opponent in check."

It was also the reason why I'd never bothered to teach anyone this technique.

"…All right, you two. Why don't we start dismembering these wolves?"

They nodded before Ireena briskly trotted up to a corpse, drawing a knife to get to work, slicing through it with her willowy fingers and a graceful flourish.

"What a waste," I unconsciously blurted out.

...Ah. Crap. I let that one slip out.

"'A waste'? What's that mean?"

"U-um, well, that's..."

Dammit! Come on, think of a good excuse... I guess I'm left with only one option.

"What I say is not to leave this dungeon," I prefaced as I knelt before one of the corpses and cast *Flare*, tinkering with the magic to transform it into the shape of a knife. "You see, if you strip the pelt a certain way, you'll make it exponentially stronger. Watch and learn."

I rammed the flaming blade into its lifeless form.

"Now, apply heat and peel off its fur. It won't look any different from (NORMAL), but its strength is staggeringly high," I explained as I trimmed away at its hide.

A transparent gray box appeared before us: **YOU OBTAINED THE FUR OF A BLACK WOLF (ULTRARARE)! VALUE: 300.**

Ireena's and Ginny's eyes widened at this announcement.

"Th-three hundred?!" Ginny shouted.

"I knew it! So there *are* levels beyond (NORMAL)."

To demonstrate the difference between (NORMAL) and (ULTRA-RARE), I scorched both these hides using *Flare*.

"Th-the normal one burned to the ground, but...!"

"Ard, how come there isn't even a single scratch on yours?!"

With wide-open eyes, the pair asked the most obvious questions first.

"H-how do you know all of this?"

"You learned it from your father, Jack, right?"

"Yep. You're right on the money, Ireena."

A total lie. One of my subordinates taught me when I was the

Demon Lord—an ex-adventurer. In fact, my underlings came from every walk of life. This one just so happened to teach me about this technique, among other things.

"Wow, I knew it. He sure is smart!"

"Um, by 'Jack,' do you mean…?"

As they continued to chatter among themselves, Ireena began picking up the hides, squirreling them away in her knapsack.

This isn't good. If she brings them back, they'll catch everyone's attention.

"Wait, Ireena. Let's toss that—" I started to say when the ground caved in and a hole gaped open beneath us.

For a moment, we were weightless.

And then everything went black.

CHAPTER 9
The Ex–Demon Lord's Lessons on Magic, Part II

…A dungeon hole was one of the many gimmicks within a labyrinth. Whenever the trap was triggered, the floor would cave in to form a yawning gap that callously tossed anyone standing there down into the lower levels—without any rhyme or reason.

That was what we'd just tumbled out from.

"Huh. I'm guessing this is…the Boss Room," I surmised, since each floor of the maze held a powerful monster known as a boss. "What is it this time? Is it a large…cow-looking person?"

"It's a M-M-M-M-Minotaur! Yep!"

A Minotaur? Seriously? *That* runty cow dude? I'd seen the real deal before, and they were mighty beasts fortified with ornate armor and magical battle-axes capable of splitting the very earth in two. Sure, this one was…um, hairy and had the head of a cow, but there were no other points of similarity between them. It wasn't even wearing armor, for crying out loud, and all it held was a dingy club.

…That said, I *guess* I could see it was the tiniest bit more challenging than a Black Wolf.

"All right. Let's bring this lesson to a close. We'll need your participation," I murmured.

"*Braaaaaaaaaaaaaaaaaaaaaghhhh!*" the beast blared, ricocheting its cries off the stone walls down through the space.

"Eeek! Eeeeeeeek…!" Ginny shrieked, looking petrified by the full force of the Minotaur's bloodlust and falling straight onto her bubble butt.

Sweat seemed to pour from her armpits and thighs as she convulsed in fear. Her blue eyes were on the brink of tears.

Ireena was in a similar state, breaking out in a cold sweat and chattering her teeth together in shock…but I didn't get it. I mean, this seemed to be an overreaction for a dinky pushover.

"All right, class. This is our final lesson on Script Magic," I declared, loping toward the Minotaur in wide strides.

"A-Ard! Please! Th-that's dangerous—," stuttered Ginny, just as it swung down its club on me.

Well, it'd tried to intimidatingly close the distance between us, but the attack was nothing to write home about, since all I had to do was use the most elementary of spells to strengthen my stats. And then I stopped it with an extended index finger.

"Mr. Minotaur," I cautioned. "At this rate, you won't even manage to squash a puny bug."

I could have just been imagining things, but it seemed to scrunch its face in irritation. I let out a little chuckle.

"Lesson number one: Never cast Script Magic at point-blank range. You'd be giving your opponent too many opportunities to attack while you're busy drawing your magic circle. It's best to keep your distance," I explained, slugging the Minotaur in the gut.

Well, I'd meant for it to be a light punch, but its oafish body soared through the air upon impact.

"N-no way…?!"

"Heh-heh-heh-heh! Nothin' to it!" exclaimed Ireena, standing tall as if she'd knocked it out herself.

Ginny had her eyes wide open with awe.

"Lesson number two: Cast your spell while your opponent is caught off guard. The results are much more dramatic that way," I continued as I swirled my finger through the air toward the crumpled beast.

As it staggered, trying to lift itself off the ground, I unleashed a *Short Flare Bomb*—calling forth a succession of explosions that swallowed its colossal body whole.

"*Braaaaaaaaaaaaaagh?!*" it howled, stumbling forward even as I mercilessly pummeled it, watching it sink into a shimmering white-hot whirlpool.

"As you can see, it's best used for attacks in rapid-fire succession, since it doesn't require any cooldown time or magical power. Plus, once your opponent is debilitated, you can continue to unleash one-sided attacks."

Our example was still engulfed in flames, totally at a loss as to where to move—or how.

Nice. Almost on the brink of death—which makes now the perfect time.

I stopped my attack and looked directly at Ginny. "Please give the finishing blow."

"...What?" she yelped, gazing at me quizzically as if she had no clue what in the hell I was saying.

I assumed a stern expression. "Think of it as a ceremony: Gather your courage and discard your past."

My eyes bored into her face, where an entire spectrum of emotions ebbed and flowed in and out of existence. It goes without saying that self-deprecation colored most of them.

I decided to give her a much-needed pep talk. "Didn't you say you wanted to change? To take center stage? Show me what you've got," I coaxed, and that led me straight to my main point. "Listen up, Ginny. Right now, your life is at a crossroads."

That seemed to spark something in her heart.

"...Up until now, I've tried to run away from all pain," she started. "I would shut myself in my room and pore over the ballads of the Demon Lord whenever I was slightly inconvenienced by anything telling myself I'd be saved one day by someone like him... even though I knew that was super pathetic."

But I don't wanna do that anymore. She might have left that unsaid, but it was clearly visible on her face.

...I knew it. She had some self-esteem.

I mean, of course she did. If we could all help it, none of us would actually *want* to be weak. In fact, we'd yank that trait right out of ourselves. She was just like me, and now, she'd managed to suppress her submissive side, draw on her confidence, and move forward—physically and psychologically.

Ginny squared off with the Minotaur, trembling and absolutely petrified of the staggering beast, even as it stood on the verge of death.

"T-take this!" she shouted, slicing the air with her finger to invoke a magic circle and releasing an infernal blow on the monster.

"*Grwaaaooooooooooooow!*" roared the Minotaur, letting out its death throes, which Ginny mistook as a raging war cry.

"*Eeeeeeeeeeeeek!*" she cried out, but her lithe fingers continued to sweep through the air and call forth attack after attack.

There was no stopping her rebirth.

The crumpling form of the hulking beast reflected in her teary eyes.

That's good. Overcome your fears. Smash your past failures, I thought.

"I've had enough! I refuse to cry! I'll become strong! I'll reinvent myself!"

Become the person you want to be.

Ginny continued to hammer the monster with blows, each accompanied by a fearsome shout—until finally, the Minotaur reached the end of its life, crumpling onto the ground like a lifeless doll.

YOU DEFEATED A MINOTAUR (NORMAL)!

It toppled over with a deafening boom that rang out, hot smoke rising off its titanic form.

"*Huh... Huh...* I-is it over...?" Ginny asked in a ragged voice, chest heaving.

When she realized she'd won, her expression softened as she fell back with a soft *thud*.

I went up to her. "Excellent work. That was splendid, Ginny," I congratulated from the bottom of my heart.

"...It's all thanks to you, Ard."

"Nonsense. The only thing I did was nudge you in the right direction. You're the one who took action. It's all you and your power, Ginny. Without a doubt."

She gazed down at her palms wordlessly. I imagined those hands seemed very different now that she'd proven her worth.

At last, she let out a giggle. "Thank you, Ard."

When she met my eyes, there wasn't a shred of doubt in them.

...I must have looked at Olivia the same way when she had saved me back then. Ginny's gaze held unlimited power and twinkled beautifully.

CHAPTER 10
The Ex–Demon Lord's Day in Review

With the whole Ginny situation finally settled, we tried to make our way back to the upper levels as we slipped out of the Boss Room, trudging through the passageway in search of a teleportation portal.

Within all labyrinths operated manually, there was always an area on each floor that allowed people to warp to any level by invoking a special technique. I prayed this dungeon wasn't some exception to the rule as we pressed onward, until eventually, we came across something peculiar.

"…What's this? A door?"

We'd stumbled onto a mysterious doorway with a massive keyhole. It was large enough to make me wonder if it was exclusively for the use of giants.

THE DOOR IS LOCKED! ITEMS NEEDED: ALUMA-TITE KEY.

…Well, it was totally useless if we couldn't open it, so we hurried on.

Nothing else worth noting happened on our little journey to the teleportation room. Yep. Everything was completely under control. When we made our safe return to the first floor, we sought out our instructor and Olivia, who were both surrounded by hordes of students who had already returned and now stared at us. They were undoubtedly expecting something big from us.

I'm sorry to say these lovely ladies and gentlemen would be sorely disappointed by our performance. I mean, we'd completely incinerated the Minotaur, which meant we couldn't strip its body for hides. It also meant I'd give perfectly average results and leave with a smile.

"Ohhhh, welcome back, you threeeee. Now, I'd like to check your furs, if you pleeeeease," our mild-mannered instructor drawled.

Ireena obliged, rummaging around to proudly draw out all three of our hides.

"Oh, this ceeeeertainly passes. This one, tooooo."

You see, even though the value of our goods had been measured and announced when we obtained them in the dungeon, there really wasn't a way to check back on those records. Meaning it was totally possible to give a false reporting of their value.

But you couldn't fool a halfling. They possessed an exclusive skill known as the Judgment Eye, which allowed them to ascertain the true value of any item. Now back to our instructor. He wasn't giving off any overexaggerated response.

Nice. I've won. I've really done it this time. Now Olivia has no reason to be suspic—

"……Oh my! Wh-whaaaat in the world is thiiiiiis…?!"

—Huh?

"Th-this one has a value of three hundred…?! D-doesn't that mean it's top claaaass?!"

…………

………

D-DAMMIIIIIIIIT!

I—I COMPLETELY FORGOT TO TOSS OUT THE SPECIAL OOOOOOOOONE!

N-no! Wait! There's still time! I can think of an excuse—

"Wh-what's the meaning of thiiiiiis?!"

"Heh-heh-heh! Ard stripped that one!" Ireena chirped.

"Yep! He used a special technique!" added Ginny.

Yoooooooooo! What the—?! Why would you tell him?! I thought we had an agreement! You promised not to tell anyone!

"A-Ard! Pleeease make me your apprentiiiice!" my instructor begged, sliding into an artful grovel.

"A special method, huh? I think I know a guy who used to talk about somethin' like that with his subordinate," Olivia noted, wearing that magnificent smile of hers as her cat ears flicked back and forth.

"I've gotta say, you have my full attention now. How about stopping by my estate later tonight, Mr. Ard?

Nooooooooo! I-I've been bumped up from first-name status to mister!!! *A-and she invited me to her estaaaaaaaate?! Th-this was it!* All my alarms bells were warning me that Olivia was thinking, *Get ready, 'cause I'm about to end you and have fun doing it!*

"How lucky... I want an invite from Lady Olivia, too..."

"A lowly commoner...?! Switch places with me, dammit...!"

Sure, be my guest! I'd be more than happy! You're gonna be the one regretting it, not me!

Aghhhh, I can't take it anymore! Why is this happening?!

Following our lesson in the dungeon, we returned to the classroom, where our homeroom teacher, Olivia, gave us a quick review of what we learned that day. With that, our lessons came to a close. If this were any normal institution, we'd break for after-school clubs by this point. But that wasn't what usually happened in a magic academy.

Well, I'd heard some whispers here and there from the girls gossiping about some secret club in the main building. But I really couldn't care less. Plus, I was pretty sure I'd never have to interact with it myself.

This all meant that I was making my way through the grounds toward the student dormitories, my home from now on. With the academic building located directly in the middle of the ginormous campus, the two dormitories were relegated to either side. One was for the exclusive use of aristocrats, the other for commoners, which meant our living quarters were arranged by status.

"Why can't Ard and I be in the same room?! Unbelievable!" Ireena huffed right before we parted ways after school.

I understood how she felt, but what can you do? Rules are rules. I pushed down the urge to go with her and said my good-byes.

After the ridiculously long walk across the school, I finally arrived at my dorm, which honestly gave me the impression that the builders had finished it with a shrug, thinking, *Eh, good enough for commoners.* Not that I had any grounds to complain. I mean, I'd stayed in *far* worse places in the past... And most importantly, it was a single-person room. That was more than enough to make me practically leap with joy.

I could imagine what would happen if I was forced to live with a roommate. All my repressed trauma would resurface, and I'd be drowning in memories of my school days when I'd spent all my time trying to hide my true form.

I didn't have much to do after I'd finished my dinner in the cafeteria, which meant that I could laze around on my bed and reflect on my first day... A lot had happened, but it could be summed up in one word: *emotional.*

My heart had been stirred, for better or worse. Olivia was definitely for worse. Without question. On the plus side...everyone had been welcoming—thankfully. It meant that I'd finally found a place for me to explore and nurture relationships with others. At this rate, I could reach my dream of making one hundred friends, so I guess it wouldn't be a "dream" for much longer. Yeah, I guess you'd be able to imagine that my first day went well. It made me hopeful for the future.

That said, I started to think when someone knocked on my door.

"Evening!" Ireena burst into the room in her negligee. "I checked with the headmaster! And guess what? He told me that commoners can't go into our dorm, but we can visit yours! Which is why…I'm here!" She threw her arms over her head, cheering as she flashed a broad smile.

I couldn't see my face right then, but I assumed I was making the same happy expression, since I could feel everything relax.

"Welcome," I said. "Please make yourself comfortable. The place is run-down, and I'm afraid I can't prepare any tea, but—"

"Oh, there's no need for any of that! I'll go anywhere as long as I'm with you, Ard!"

…Gah. That struck me harder than any divine punishment could.

We plopped down on the bed, chatting up a storm, and before we knew it, the clock was ticking past ten. You know what they say: Time flies when you're having fun.

"Ireena, you should return soon."

"…Can I sleep here with you?" she asked, tugging gently on my sleeve, looking up at me with her big eyes, and pleading demurely.

It was supereffective.

"If I can't sleep with you, I'll be too lonely to sleep at all…"

And who could say no after hearing that?

I expressed my consent, turning out the light before we climbed into bed.

"I apologize for the cramped quarters."

"It's fine. I love snuggling right next to you," she admitted somewhat bashfully, drawing my left arm closer to her to pad her head while she totally looked like a sweet angel.

Since my room was supplied with a bed meant for one person, it was almost like every inch of our bodies was touching. I mean, I was basically cradling her in my arms, which also meant that I was fully assaulted by her feminine softness and faint floral fragrance wafting off her warm body. Oh, and did I mention her chest? Her full breasts were pushed up against me, spilling onto my side of the bed with every breath, molding themselves against my chest. The gentle sensuality of her body pressed against mine was making me acutely aware of her womanhood.

Her breasts, both firm and supple as freshly made mochi; her breaths blowing agonizingly close against the back of my neck; her snowy, plump thighs wound around my legs; her seductive, feminine scent.

With all that said, it wasn't like I harbored even a fraction of carnal desire for Ireena. After all, she was my good friend. Weiss had entrusted me with her care, and I saw her as my beloved daughter. All of this meant that I could never make her the target of these repulsive thoughts.

"Zzz, zzz...... I wuuuuve you, Awd...," she innocently mumbled in her sleep.

We were friends. That was it. My feelings were purely platonic.

I stroked her lovely silver hair, breaking into a soft smile, and then returned to the thought that'd been running through my mind.

If I can keep this act up, I bet I can make tons of friends. But if they were to ever uncover the whole truth, everyone would distance themselves from me.

It would be a repeat of my previous life when my former friends became my subordinates. They'd treat me as a monster. They'd look at me with fear in their eyes. Just like Elrado.

Ireena would be no different, I bet. My mouth hardened at the thought of it. *I don't ever want this girl to fear me. I don't ever want to let something precious slip away from me ever again.*

To make sure that would never come to pass, I vowed I wouldn't do anything that would draw undue attention to myself from here on out.

...Fast-forward to a few days following that promise.

I'd been called in by the headmaster for some reason or another. I made my way to his office after school, finding Count Golde waiting in front of his desk—and Olivia, who haughtily gazed down at me.

"Thanks for coming, Ard! I've heard many tales about your performance in class! Wonderful! Wonderful! I reckon you'll make it into our history books, young man!"

I'm begging you to stop, lest her smile get bigger or more delighted.

"What business might you have with me today?"

"Right, about that. Did you know we host a battle event every spring for the students?"

"This is the first I've heard of it."

"Hmm. I see, I see. Well, not to worry," he consoled, fiddling with his beard. "Anyhoo. I've got a little favor to ask, Ard."

"...What might that be?" I asked cautiously, feeling some dread simmering inside me.

But I tried to tell myself it was my imagination.

Back to his request. Drum roll, please.

"Participate in the next battle event and put on a marvelous performance!"

...............HA-HA-HA! CAN YOU BELIEVE THIS GUY?!

HA-HA-HA!

HA-HA-HA!

HA-HA-HA-HA-HA-HA-HA-HA-HA-HA!

NO!   WAY   IN!   HELL!

CHAPTER 11
The Ex–Demon Lord and an Invitation

Participate in a school-sponsored event? And smash the competition? Thanks, but no thanks. I didn't want to stick out more than I already had or...give Olivia any more room for suspicion. That left me with one choice.

"I cast spells to help those in need. It's not my style to flaunt them before the masses at a public exhibition."

...Which is why I politely decline your request, I wanted to say.

"That is very noble of you. Yes, very noble. But if that's what's holding you back, well, I have to admit, I've got plenty of cause for concern."

"...What do you mean?"

Golde toyed with his chin hairs. "Well, it's hard to talk about, but our alums and current students haven't really done anything to write home about. From my perspective, I'm simply happy that our country is peaceful enough to not need their help, but...it's a different story from *their* perspective. You know, the government."

...Ah, I see. So that's where this is going.

"As I'm sure you're aware, this school belongs to them, meaning they control our purse strings. What I'm tryin' to say is..."

"If the state decides there's no more use for you, they'll cut your budget without hesitation…which makes this event an appeal to increase funds."

"Right. You're a bright one, Ard. Very perceptive. The royal family started the tradition of the student battle, and members of the country's upper crust all come out to see it. If we can get on their good side by showing off a star student, the government would have no choice but to give us a steady stream of income."

"…In other words, you're telling me to be your cash cow, right?"

"No, no, no! It's nothing as evil as that! I'm just always thinking of the future of the academy and its students—figured a little more spending money will do us all a bit of good!" Golde bowed his head entreatingly. "Look at me! Please! Please, oh, please help us out!"

If I could have just given him a flat-out no, life would be so much easier. But you've got to remember that with age comes pride—even more so when you've got power, like Golde. Plus, I was some lowly commoner, and he was a count. And on top of that, he was bowing to *me*.

I had to take all that into consideration, even though I didn't want to stand out.

"…Please raise your head. May I have some time to think it over?"

"Of course. We've still got time until the opening ceremony. Let us know when you're ready."

Well, I guess that was that. I spun on my heel and made a beeline for the door.

"'Magic exists to help those in need,' was it? I think I might have had a stupid brother who used to spout the same drivel," noted Olivia.

I was pretty sure I could guess who this "stupid brother" was. That said, it was generic, cliché even, and nothing that linked me directly to the Demon Lord.

"Hey, son of the Great Mages. Humor me by listening to my little monologue, won't you?"

Olivia continued on before I could answer.

"I used to act all high-and-mighty toward my stupid little brother—never showing him any affection...even though I'd always respected him in my heart... You know what? I even loved him. I would have died for him."

...I knew as much. I'd felt the same way. I would have thrown my life away for Olivia's sake.

"That's why... That's why I have to see him again."

"...To punish the traitorous Demon Lord for reincarnating into some other life-form without discussing it with you beforehand?"

"No, that's not it. I want to...apologize to him."

"Huh?" That caught me off guard.

Not that she noticed. Olivia's cat ears were back and flat against her head.

"It's my fault that he reincarnated. After all, I'd left him to his own devices, alone in the world. That's what drove him to do such a thing. Betrayal. But I had my reasons, too, you know. I want to talk to him about it and apologize...to go back to the way things used to be between us. To laugh together over nothing, just like siblings. That's how I really feel."

These curveballs left me speechless. My eyes started to well with tears, clouding over my vision. I never knew that she felt this way. I'd been sure she would unleash her fury once she found me out, but that didn't appear to be the case after all.

She was kinder than anyone else. How could I forget? She would never, ever attempt to live long enough just to punish her little brother.

How had she felt when those boundaries sprang up between us back then? The line that separated us into subordinate and superior. Now that I was reflecting on it, I realized I'd treated her like a traitor, but never once asked her how she felt about the matter... I'd acted like a complete child.

"Lady Olivia..."

I had to say it. I had to tell her I was the Demon Lord. Then we could be a family again—

"Yes. I'll make up with him...then get revenge for my steamed potato...!"

"Um? ...What? E-erm. What do you mean...?"

"What do I mean? That piece of garbage ate *my* delicious potato that I'd been saving for myself, and then he had the *gall* to reincarnate himself to skedaddle on out of there...!"

...Damn, that's right. I totally forgot. I wolfed down her potato at the very last second to piss her off. I figured I'd never see her again... I can't believe it's come back to bite me...!

"I'll never forget my frustration and hatred! That's why I'm gonna find him and make him pay! That's why I've lived on for thousands of years!"

What kind of life is that? Geez, what a face. You don't look like a demon. You are *a bloody demon.*

Thank goodness I hadn't admitted the truth. I was better off never admitting it at all. I'd been the one to instigate it, I guess; I wasn't ready to deal with the repercussions in the slightest.

I was about to just put the lid back on this can of worms.

"I'm sure I'll figure out exactly who and what you are in the upcoming events, O son of the Great Mages" she predicted, her voice dripping with suspicion. I bet she'd already pinned my identity down by this point.

Now I had to deal with her on top of this event? Gimme a break. As I broke into a cold sweat, I hurried out of the room.

Ireena was waiting outside for me. Her seriously cherubic face eased some of my mounting tension as we made our way back toward the dormitories. But I was still racking my brain, looking for a way to get out of this tournament.

First things first, Golde wanted me to participate to obtain *more funding for the academy.* If that was the end goal, that meant I wouldn't need to show up to the event if we could procure it using other means.

Of all the high-ranking officials, it was the queen who had the firmest grasp on the nation's purse strings. If we could negotiate with the queen, that would be ideal, since the government veered close to an absolute monarchy. But even if that were in the realm of possibilities, we wouldn't be able to sway her decision since we had no real bargaining chips. That all meant we needed to obtain leverage first and then find a way to get a seat at the negotiating table.

And the real problem is figuring out how to secure both these things, I thought as Ireena and I exited the building.

"Oh, Ard!" cooed a familiar voice.

I whipped around to find a certain someone beaming up at me.

It was Ginny. She let her medium-length peach hair sway and barely covered boobs bounce up and down as she trotted over to us.

As she skidded to a stop, she looked at me imploringly. "Any plans for our day off tomorrow?"

"No, nothing in particular."

"In that case...p-please go on a date with me!"

...Huh? A date? A date date? Like for lovers? But we aren't in that kind of relationship... Oh, wait. Could it be about that incident from before? Huh, I guess Ginny's fallen in love with— No, stop that. Don't jump to conclusions. You've been burned enough times in your past life, haven't you? This is what they call..."leading you on." Yeah, that's totally it. Women are just like that.

I'd been in a similar situation way back when I'd attempted to conceal my true form at my previous academy. On top of being completely friendless, I was called a certain number of things: "that thing in the corner" or "that idiot with middle-parted hair" or "that gloomy baldy" were a choice few.

But there was one girl who took notice of me. With her kindness and ravishing good looks, it was really no wonder she'd been the most popular girl in school. Which meant she wasn't exclusively kind to just me, but…it made me feel a certain way. At the time, I was totally inexperienced in love and became completely obsessed with her. I wouldn't have realized in a million years that she was leading me on. When I took matters into my own hands and finally confessed…well, I'm sure you already know what happened.

"Oh, I like you, too…less than I like goblins," she replied thoughtfully.

There'd been a reason why she was called the belle of the school. I mean, she'd fully managed to sidestep the word *hate* and still obliterate my dreams.

That said, damn. Less than a goblin, huh? I guess she really did hate me.

Oh, and after the whole debacle, she was still kind to everyone— well, everyone except me.

"A-Ard? Wh-why are you crying?"

"It's nothing. Just some gunk that got in my eye—gunk called 'memories.'"

For a moment, Ginny recoiled in surprise, but she snapped back to her normal self relatively quickly. "W-well, then! Back to what I was saying earlier!" she continued, gazing up at me with hope in her eyes.

I was seriously confused. I had no idea what this girl was thinking. How could I even respond?

…I couldn't refuse. She'd be devastated… That meant there was really only one answer.

"Understood. I'll accompany you tomorrow."

"Whaaaaat?! Really?! Hooray!" Ginny cheered and hopped around excitedly. Her hair and ample assets moved in perfect sync.

"W-waiiiiiiiit a second!" screeched Ireena.

She was as surprised as everyone else that she'd raised her voice, and her beauty was marred by horrible confusion for a minute, but then she focused her gaze on Ginny in a scowl.

"M-me too! I'm going, too!" she exclaimed as her long silvery hair bristled like a dog's tail.

She was trying her best to come off as intimidating.

However, Ginny had been keeping up her cheerful smile the entire time. "Of course! That's perfectly fine by me!"

Ireena clearly didn't expect her to agree so easily, cocking her head and regarding Ginny with a quizzical look. "R-really?"

"Sure. I don't intend to keep him all to myself. I mean, I think Ard should have a harem of girls! You and I can be girls one and two; then we can build up from there!"

Erm, a harem is…not my style. Plus, I hate the word itself. It brings back too many bad memories.

In my old life, I'd somehow amassed a different kind of harem (for troublemakers exclusively), and because of that…

Nope. I'm not going there right now. No need to dig up repressed thoughts.

As that swirled through my mind, Ireena tilted her head adorably. "Hey, Ard. What's a *hair-em*?"

…Oh, Ireena. My pure, sweet maiden. Of course she wouldn't know about this. There was no way in hell I was going to make this a teachable moment, either. All I wanted was for her to stay the way she was and—

"Well, a harem is…," Ginny started to explain, completely trampling on my wishes as she slunk over to Ireena and whispered in her ear.

I bet she went into the fine details, too, because Ireena's ivory complexion became redder and redder until it resembled a perfectly ripe apple.

"Wh-wh-wh-wh-wh-wha…?! N-no way! Absolutely not! Forget it! I will never, ever allow this 'harem' thing to happen!"

"…Whaaat? Awww, why not?"

"Because it's disgusting! Ard surrounded by a bunch of girls?! Just thinking about it makes me sick!"

"…Makes you sick? Really? But wouldn't it be so cool?" Ginny prompted.

"I don't get how that could possibly be 'cool'! I mean, Ard is *my* friend and mine alone! Even thinking about all those girls…makes me so mad! No way I'm allowing this! And that's that!" she huffed, inflating her cheeks in a fit of adorable anger and looking like the very definition of an angel.

Ginny never let go of her grin. "Ohhh, I see. Well, to each her own, I suppose."

…My eyes must have been playing tricks on me, but I swore I could see something miasmic, something pitch-black swirling behind Ginny…

"That aside, we have a date to plan! Just think about how to let Ard have some fun, okay?" Ginny suggested before bowing elegantly and taking her leave with her chest held high. "How should I get rid of Miss Ireena?"

…I thought I'd heard that last bit, but it was probably my imagination.

I left the dormitory for commoners the following morning, heading straight for the school gate, our proposed meet-up spot. It made getting together easier since Ireena and Ginny were living in the dorms on campus, too.

"Oh, Ard! Good morn—"

"Good morning, Ard!" Ginny interrupted, barreling past Ireena to step out in front of her.

"Hrrrgh…!" Ireena was none too happy about it, cheeks puffed out in endearing protest.

But Ginny paid her no mind and trotted up to me. "What do you think? I bought this outfit just for today... How is it?"

"Y-you look nice," I replied honestly.

Her all-white attire made her seem sweet and innocent. That said, it was revealing enough to draw attention to her cleavage... And I felt incredibly turned on, though that could have been due to her powers as a succubus.

"Hmm? My eyes are up here?"

"Huh? Ah, no, I..."

"Hee-hee-hee. You just can't get enough of me," she said coyly, giggling with a dainty hand over her mouth and acting devilishly seductive.

Ginny stole a glance at Ireena in her uniform. I guessed that the date was too short notice for her to prepare anything fancier.

"...I win the first round," she muttered, which fired up Ireena's competitive spirit.

She shot Ginny a fierce look. "*What?!* Won in what way?!"

"Hmm? Did I say something? I can't seem to remember..." Ginny continued to feign innocence.

Ireena growled.

...That's strange. Aren't dates supposed to be fun? All I'm feeling is a stomachache.

"Well then, let us be off, Ard!"

"Wh-what are you grabbing his arm for?! Quit acting so cozy!"

Squeezed between two girls who were at each other's throats, I set off on my first date.

CHAPTER 12
The Ex–Demon Lord and His First Date Ever

Ginny planned to take us on a tour of the royal capital for our three-way date, guiding us through a few landmarks, since I was unfamiliar with the city. In all honesty, she was doing a better job than I'd expected, providing us with actual pointers and facts.

All the while, passersby stared at us.

I supposed that was unavoidable. After all, they saw a dignified boy wandering around with two gorgeous girls. But their envious glares didn't get to my head or anything. There was a particular reason for that.

"The palace is a must-see, right?! Who cares about the dumb old library?!"

"Oh-ho-ho. You don't get him at all, Miss Ireena. And to think you want him all to yourself. Listen up. Ard is an intellectual—unlike you. How could you expect him to be interested in the palace of all things? It's knowledge that moves him the most. Right, Ard?"

"Huh? N-no, that's, uh."

"You wanna see the palace! You can't wait to see its huge, sparkly amazingness, right?!"

"U-um, that's, uh."

This had been going on for a while now. My stomach was seriously killing me.

…Fast-forward to us finishing our tour and entering the theater for part two of our date. Watching a performance was a pretty standard activity, or so I'd heard.

The show began shortly after we reached our seats.

All plays had their standard plotlines, no matter the era or location. The Laville Empire of Sorcery was no exception, and we had two go-tos: first, the ballad of the Demon Lord, though this story line wasn't exclusive to our country. Second, a story based on the legends leading up to the founding of our nation.

Apparently, the predecessor of our current state was an empire that had been destroyed by a white dragon named Elzard. Known as the "Frenzied King of Dragons," it had pushed humanity to the brink of collapse, but one young man was able to put a stop to its diabolical scheme, restoring peace on earth. After that, he'd become the first emperor. Well, that was a very simplified version of those events, and now it was being performed on the stage in front of us.

The scenes depicting the atrocities committed by the King of Dragons were needlessly intense and, to be honest, a little petrifying. Beside me, Ireena must have felt the same way, because she was sweating buckets.

"Oh, Miss Ireena, you're covered in sweat. Are you that frightened?"

"Wh-wh-wh-what are you talking about?! I-I-I-I'm not scared at all! N-no King of Dragons can s-s-s-scare me!" she asserted in absolute fear.

As I internally doted on her, the second half of the play began, focusing on…the ballad of the heroic Demon Lord.

"I am the Almighty King Varvatos! Evil Gods, ready yourselves! Your tyrannical reign shall come to an end—today!"

The performance began to recount the part where Megisa del Sol, one of the Evil Gods, or the "Outer Ones" in ancient times, was vanquished. I'd spent half my past life fighting these guys.

Produce more demons, control humanity, treat them like slaves: That was modus operandi for the Outer Ones' reign of tyranny, but I'd wanted to create a world where we determined and carved out history with our own hands.

As someone born with nothing, I latched on to that ideal, eventually forming a rebel army with Olivia and declaring war on the world. After a series of twists and turns, the Evil Gods were sealed away, for the most part, or sent back to their original world.

With that said, the glory was in no way all mine. I had irreplaceable comrades who both fought and fell alongside me in battle. The Evil Gods would have never been eradicated without their help... They were all such great people that I could never rank them against one another.

However, *a certain person* in particular will forever hold a special place deep in my heart.

"You always do as you please! Stop leaving me hanging by a thread!" called out the actress onstage.

"...Lydia."

Lydia had rejected the Outer Ones and fought to put the world back in humanity's hands, just like me. But our methods diverged slightly—causing us to butt heads on more than a few occasions. Back then, her group had been denounced as traitors, but in the current world, she was shown as an example of heroism and given the title of Champion.

"I admit that you can call on immense power, but please! Rely on me a little more!"

"Right, sorry. I won't let it happen again."

As I observed the actress and actor have this exchange onstage as Lydia and my former self, respectively, it involuntarily brought back a huge wave of old memories, causing a full-body shiver down my spine. Well, more accurately...my body trembled in *rage*. I couldn't believe how many artistic liberties the playwrights had taken to distort her character out of proportion.

I mean, come on. They put that meathead in a position to admonish *me*.

Of course, I knew it'd be impossible for a play to accurately pin down every single character and line. It couldn't be 100 percent true to history. But, like, this was too much, especially if you consider that these characters totally swapped our actual personalities.

Back in the day, that king of fools was constantly throwing a wrench in my plans...

"H-hey! Wait! Stop! If you rush in now, all our plans will be—"

"Shut up! Here I come, you bastaaaaaaaaards!"

Just like that. And every single time she ruined one of my plans, I always had to reprimand her...

"Look before you leap, idiot! It's a complete mystery to me how you're going about like nothing ever happened! Quit acting like a dumb-ass!"

"Whaaaaaaat?! Who you callin' an idiot, moron?! Say that again—I dare ya!"

She'd get pissed off when I yelled at her for being reckless, and then she'd punch me for it... How I ever became friends with that raging fool was the greatest mystery of my past life.

Oh, and speaking of personality changes, the actions and behaviors of the Four Heavenly Kings ended up unintentionally hilarious. Seriously. The playwrights were idealizing them a little too much, no? They were nothing like the saints onstage. I mean, they were a tough crowd to wrangle as subordinates.

For starters, the strongest of the Heavenly Kings, Alvarto, was a messed-up war nut.

As for the self-proclaimed "genius scholar," Verda was a dirty little mad scientist.

And then, there was Lizer, who seemed decent at first glance, until you realized that he was a twisted lolicon.

Last but not least, my big sister, Olivia, was the grossest of all with her full-on brother complex.

"Ah, my dear king. To your good health," said an actor.

Alvarto would never have said that. It would've been more like, *Ah, my dear king. To your sudden death.* Yep, that sounded about right.

"Your Highness! I, Verda, may be unworthy, but I have invented a new form of magic!"

That sounds nothing like Verda. Try: *"Hey! Hey, Var! Your favorite genius came up with somethin' supercool, so come be my guinea pig! Pleeeeease? It'll be totally fine! You'll just go a li'l insane is all!"* Yeah, that's much better.

"Your Majesty. I would like you to review the new laws. The Council of Seven and I have made a few amendments that need your review."

Wrong again. Lizer would say, *"Your Majesty. The Council of Seven's nitpicking the shit out of my law. It's supposed to be for the benefit of little girls. I'm requesting your permission to destroy them."* Just like that.

"Please be at ease and allow me to handle this. I'll always have your back."

As for Olivia… Well, other than her tone of voice, this play wasn't too far off. But when I let her "have my back" or whatever, she'd secretly snip off some of my hairs for her private collection, among other things… What I'm trying to say is that on the outside, she played the part of a peerless beauty. On the inside, she was rotten to the core.

Anyway, neither Ginny nor Ireena knew the truth, and from the looks of it, they were enjoying the play just like everyone else, especially the tale of Rivelg, the knight of roses, which brought them both to tears.

In this episode, the knight meets a tragic end while trying to save a girl who had been taken hostage, as he's tricked by the despicable followers of God and revolts against the Demon Lord, breaking his allegiance with him.

That was how the story supposedly went...but once again, the truth had gotten distorted. But this was inevitable. After all, I'd made it that way. I'd felt disappointed in his desperate revolt against me... But to preserve his legacy, I gave strict orders to prevent the truth from ever getting out into world.

Recalling those events made me think about when exactly Rivelg had started planning his rebellion. There was a particular time that came to mind.

He'd been one of my close associates, strong enough to be the captain of the guard and well-versed in governance. He had incredible talent, you see.

But on that fateful day, Rivelg had stared daggers in my direction for no reason, right as I had some business to go over with Olivia. That was the moment I thought I had realized his true feelings: that he was infatuated with Olivia.

At the time, I welcomed this revelation with arms flung wide open. I had thought it was about time for Olivia to settle down, and I figured having him around meant she'd finally let go of her little brother. But Rivelg couldn't help but doubt the nature of my relationship with her. In order to rectify this, I had set up a place for us to talk alone at a later date.

"D-did you have some business with me?"

"Yeah. I thought I'd clear up a little misunderstanding on your part. I don't have the relationship you think I do with Olivia. It's nothing like that at all."

"I-is that true?"

It looked like a huge weight had been lifted off his shoulders. He must have really liked her.

"Yes. Y'know, Rivelg... You're an open book."

"Wha—?!" His eyes widened in horror, his face slick with a cold sweat. "D-do you…?! D-do you see right through me, Your Majesty…?!"

"Aye. Furthermore, Rivelg, I accept your feelings."

"Hghwa?!"

I'd never heard such a sound before. I guessed I'd never realized how even the coolest and most collected men could become all mushy-gushy in love and I reveled in this new discovery.

"I know I can trust you," I continued with bravado. "After all, I've got nothing but praise for your academic and military performances—and your character. Even among my subordinates, you've clearly got some serious talent. Rivelg, you have my total confidence."

"Y-Your Majesty…! I knew it was the right choice to pledge my loyalty to you for the past hundred years…!" he exclaimed, working himself up to the point that he started to weep.

Well, he'd always been one to jump to conclusions. I mean, at that point, we still hadn't known whether Olivia held any special feelings toward Rivelg, and I'd been getting ready to point that out, but then he beat me to the punch.

"To think the day would come when His Majesty's *sweet ass* would finally be mine…!"

"………Huh?"

I could remember this exact moment like it was yesterday, especially the part when I'd become completely awash with the very distinct sensation of *What the hell is this guy going on about?*

"W-wait. I'm talking about entrusting Olivia to you," I'd clarified.

"…Huh? U-um, but didn't you say you could see through my feelings, Your Majesty?"

"You like Olivia, don't you?"

Please say yes. I'm begging you, I'd pleaded internally… But my wishes had been instantly pulverized.

"N-no, you've got it all wrong! Um, I guess this is my opportunity to say it loud and clear... I'm completely enamored by you—and your butt, Your Majesty!"

At the time, I had absolutely no idea how to respond.

I could say I'd had my fair share of experiences, but this was the first time my mind completely blanked out. My response flew out of my mouth just based on pure instinct.

"No. Absolutely not."

And that...had led to Rivelg's uprising.

The whole thing had been truly unfortunate. A disaster. I guess it just goes to show that you never really know anyone. I mean, I had no idea he was gay.

Sure, he was sickly sweet to handsome young men and ogled the asses of brawny knights as he smacked his lips, but I'd never suspected he was interested in men.

"Awww, poor Sir Rivelg..."

"To die with the one you love in your arms... How tragic..."

Those two sobbed along with the other guests... I felt like crying, too. For more reasons than one.

Ginny didn't waste a single beat to snake her arm around mine when we stepped out of the theater.

"The play was packed with super-interesting stories!"

If I was being totally honest with her, I would have vigorously shaken my head. But I did my best to respond appropriately and obligingly nod in response.

Ginny blushed. "But I bet I wouldn't have enjoyed myself if I went alone. I wonder if it was because you were there with me...? Hee-hee-hee, just kidding," she teased, sticking her tongue out with a bashful little grin.

She was acting all cutesy...which made blood rush to my cheeks all of a sudden.

Is she really just leading me on? I was starting to wonder if she actually had the hots for me. That said… I'd have no idea how to respond or act if that was true. I mean, I've always been the one in pursuit when it came to romance… Or no, wait. There was one exception to the rule.

There was a female general who readily came to mind. I'd beaten her in some competition or battle, and she'd come up to me, saying all kinds of stuff, like *"I fell in love with your majestic figure at first sight…"* Well, I guess I'm not sure if she actually liked me. Just read one of her love letters, and you'll understand.

To my beloved Demon Lord,

I've heard news of your successes and prosperity over recent months, Your Majesty. **Still, I'm way stronger than you.**

I've noticed it's gotten chillier lately. How are you faring? **I'm powerful as always, thanks.**

The hunting season is drawing near again, and it feels like only yesterday that I gazed upon your brilliance when you landed the first mark. I'm hopeful you will reign supreme again, but **don't forget that I can overcome you at any time.**

During the competition last year, you were virile and gallant, completely captivating the entire stadium, Your Majesty. But I hope you will always remember the name of the one who was most bewitched. It was I, Freya, Your Highness. My heart beats faster than everyone else's, and if you would allow me to mention one more thing—

Remember that if I go all out, I'll always be better than you.

I hope you and I, **the almighty Freya,** *can engage in some friendly competition once again this year.*

With all my love.

Best **(in class),**

The World's Strongest Woman

Freya

…My army had been extremely talented and equally full of oddballs and perverts.

"Let's go find somewhere to eat! You could use some food, right?" Ginny purred.

I nodded.

"I know just the place! I looked it up for today!" She grinned, tugging on my arm and drawing it closer to her enormous breasts.

I could feel them jiggle and mold themselves around my arm.

...Hold up. Is she not wearing a bra?

"Hmm? What's the matter? Are you blushing?" Ginny giggled coyly, the spitting image of a coquette.

...I give up. I had absolutely no clue how to respond, especially since I'd never dealt with this sort of thing before. But my behavior seemed to give Ireena the wrong idea.

"C'mon, knock it off! Let's get going already!" she snapped, yanking my arm and tearing me away from Ginny's grasp.

It was kind of like an older sister refusing to let the younger one monopolize their big brother's time, which was absolutely adorable. *Geez, she's seriously the cutest—*

"...Tch. I knew Miss Ireena would be a pain."

I thought I heard a wicked voice right beside me, but it must have been my imagination.

"Let's go! Their curry is the best, y'know? Oh-ho-ho-ho!" Ginny said.

Yep, definitely my imagination. There's no way this pure, innocent girl could be evil, I thought as we continued to chat, strolling down the main road. That's when something caught my interest.

"Damn, she's one stubborn woman..."

"No wonder they tout her as a messenger of the Holy Goddess or whatever."

"Well, when it comes down to it, the queen is only human. I say it's high time."

There were some low murmurs coming from the backstreets, an

odd conversation between those concealed in black robes and looking clearly suspicious. Ireena and Ginny seemed to pick up on this, too.

"Those guys seem sketchy, right?"

"I swear I heard them say the queen is stubborn... It sounds like they're trying to assassinate her or something..."

Alongside the pair, I dubiously examined the alleyway gathering again.

"Well, she's in for a real treat when we complete that magic circle... Come on, let's get a move on," ordered a man—probably their leader—and the shady group obliged.

"What should we do? I'm planning on following them, of course," I said, especially because who knew if this would develop into a super-serious problem down the line?

There was no way we could ignore this. Plus...I couldn't let this one slide for personal reasons. If we ended up stopping a crime syndicate from assassinating the queen, we'd be able to use that as a bargaining chip, meaning a direct audience with her and a chance to secure more funds for the academy. Of course, the ultimate goal was to decline appearing in that annoying-ass battle event.

"I'm coming with you, Ard. I can't let anything happen to the queen," Ireena declared.

"Same. I think I can actually make a difference now," Ginny continued.

They both nodded with steadfast resolve as we immediately started coming up with a plan to track down the suspicious group.

CHAPTER 13
The Ex–Demon Lord in Pursuit

The three of us inconspicuously shadowed the group, maintaining a safe distance between us and slinking behind them in silence through the winding backstreets until they disappeared down into a manhole.

"The sewer, huh. I suppose that would be the most appropriate place to scheme in secret."

Something was beginning to stink all right.

We shot one another a glance, giving a single nod, and entered the manhole, noticing the magic-powered torches fixed to the walls at even intervals that granted us clear vision underground. We quietly tiptoed farther and farther inside until the group in black robes came into view.

They'd halted right before a wall with a humongous special-class magic circle scribbled on it. As soon as I deciphered their magical formula, I instantly understood what they were trying to do.

"Ah, I see. That's what's going on. We're—"

In the midst of my sentence, a voice interrupted me from behind with a stern warning.

"Don't move or I'll kill you."

That caused Ireena and Ginny to tremble from head to toe. As for me, I was internally mumbling to myself that I knew this would happen as I turned around toward the voice and found about a dozen men and women in the tunnels. These guys weren't in black robes, but I could guess they were all comrades based on their behavior.

"Well, well. Hook, line, and sinker." One of the figures at the front of the circle snickered, forming a smile on his severe features. This was the one I'd marked as their leader earlier.

"I'll say it one more time: No funny business, all right? Your life is completely in our hands. Once we cast the attack spell with this special-class magic circle, you'll be sent writhing into the bowels of hell."

Ireena and Ginny both went pale at this threat in silence, completely slick with sweat. Their bodies quivered, and terror filled their eyes. On the other hand, I felt his monologue was terribly cliché and let a laugh slip out.

"You think this is funny? I gotta say, that's pretty ballsy. Don't you realize you're about to die?" he hissed, seemingly ready to kill at a moment's notice.

I answered with a casual retort. "I beg to differ. Two reasons: One, you appear to have no intention of ending us. If you did, there'd be no need to surround us and blabber on and on. A surprise attack would have been enough."

I stared pointedly at the leader and continued.

"By luring us from the very start and meticulously preparing a special-class magic circle, one can assume you intended to take either one or all of us as hostages. This is only my first reason. Second—"

Before I could finish my sentence, the magic circle on the wall glowed brightly—and, in a single moment, engulfed my entire body in flames, scorching my flesh from the inside out and raging as if threatening to burn it to nothing.

"A-Ard?!"

"No, Ard!"

Wow, to think that even their screams would be nearly identical.

A man's crude laughter was thrown into the mix.

"Ha-ha! You were only half-right! Sure, we never planned on killing you, but nothin' says we have to keep anything besides the target alive, either. That means I'm free to kill annoying-ass brats like you!"

I see. Well, since he had the upper hand, I guess it was understandable how my attitude from earlier might have been unpleasant, since failing to show deference could be taken as an insult. It seemed that the man's compatriots shared his feelings, as a few chuckles went up here and there.

But those grins disappeared in a matter of seconds, and looks of terror took their place.

"...How is he still standing? He should be completely incinerated by now," said someone in the group.

I calmly provided an answer. "Why wouldn't I be standing? I'm still alive."

The place fell into an uproar.

"Wha—?! D-did he just speak?!"

"Th-that's impossible! His guts should be cooked from the inside out!"

I chuckled. "You didn't let me finish. I'll tell you the second reason why I'm not afraid. It's simple. Your strategy is no threat to me whatsoever. This is like a dozen or so ants teaming up against a lion. Nothing to be scared of," I declared as I summoned some defensive magic to extinguish the irritating flames that clung to my body.

And of course, I replaced my incinerated clothes with a molecular conversion spell.

"Hmph. I guess there are some flames inside," I observed.

Each time my mouth opened, I belched out smoke, and it was seriously starting to make me feel sick.

It would seem that I'd continue to burn as long as that magic circle was in place, which was starting to get on my nerves. I pointed a finger at it, and a geometric pattern immediately appeared at my fingertips, shooting out a single bolt of purple light and crashing into the target. A part of the circle burst violently, snuffing out the flames inside me.

"Q-quit screwin' around…! H-h-how in the world did you…?!"

"It's simple. If my body continues to burn, I merely have to keep healing it. That's all there is to it."

This was yawn-worthy from my perspective, but I guess the idea went far beyond their wildest imaginations.

"Are you trying to tell me that he can heal his body at the same speed as it burns? All without chanting an incantation?"

"Th-that's impossible! H-he should have been burned to a crisp by now! If his innards have been cooking this long, he should be going mad with pain!"

What? Really, now? Go mad from this? This era was full of nothing but a bunch of wimps. I mean, the soldiers of ancient times would have never shown weakness over something like charred intestines… But I guessed I'd save that for another day.

"S-stay calm! There are only three of them and dozens of us! We've got the upper hand here!" boomed their leader.

True, he'd be right based on the standards of his time. After all, their mages could cast only one spell at a time. That meant they could easily be defeated when taking on multiple enemies solo. Of course, it'd be a completely different story if one of the mages was terribly overpowered. But even then, I'd heard here and there that twenty average dudes could defeat even a master mage. That holds true only with people in this generation, though.

"All right. I don't have enough time in the world to deal with small fries forever. I'm itching to get this over with already, which means—" I halted, snapping my fingers together sharply to call forth a bunch of magic circles above the group.

A sudden burst of purple lightning showered down from overhead, striking the conspirators with devastating blows one after another—as you can see, there's no such thing as safety in numbers against me, the Demon Lord.

As I heaved a big sigh, I took stock of my fallen enemies—well, all except one. There was a single person still standing on his own two feet: their apparent leader, who was glaring at me menacingly.

"I purposefully saved you for last. I won't be able to sleep tonight if I don't know the reason why you targeted us. If you cooperate and confess, we can wrap this up without any more needless violence."

"Ngh…! Y-you're a monster!" he barked back, the last snarl of a sore loser.

Well, it didn't look like he was planning on confessing anytime soon. What a massive pain in the ass. That said, this would be over and done with if I cast a spell to brainwash him.

"Well, let's start with the very beginning," I suggested, approaching him slowly with a smile.

"Ngh…! As if I'd just sit by and let everything go your way!" he shouted, apparently planning to resist to the bitter end. He stood on guard as his entire body assumed an offensive stance.

And then, what I had assumed would be a futile gesture of defiance against me went well beyond my expectations.

"Ggghhhh…! *Gu-go-gaaaaaaaaaaaaaaaah!*"

With a bloodcurdling scream, he was completely enveloped in a pitch-back aura.

And then he began to transform.

CHAPTER 14

The Ex–Demon Lord and a Confrontation with the Demons

Crack. Splat. As sounds of his transformation echoed though the space, the man morphed into something else entirely. And even though he'd been the one to accuse me of being a monster a few moments earlier, it was now safe to say that he was the one who had been hiding under the guise of a human.

Two horns sprouted from his head, a pair of wings sprang from his back, and golden fur covered every inch of his skin. He began to take a similar shape to that of a Minotaur.

"*H-hwaaaah?!*"

"*A d-demon?!*"

Ginny and Ireena shrieked in unison.

Yeah, it seemed he was a demon after all, though I couldn't say for sure whether his gang members were his kin or just brainwashed humans. But back to business.

"If you want to challenge me, I accept. Come at me," I declared.

Either way, it wouldn't change the course of my actions. I was fully ready to take him on.

"*Lightning Burst!* Ngh!" he howled, but I could hear the fear in his voice.

As if to drive this point home, his attack spell blasted upward, completely missing me and puncturing the ceiling with a torrent of gigantic lightning bolts. Once he created a gaping hole leading from the sewers to the surface, he batted his wings and launched himself out of the tunnel.

"D-did he run away...?"

"I-it seems so."

I called out to the relieved girls. "I'm gonna chase after him. As for the guys on the floor, let's just let them be for now. I'm guessing they won't have any intel anyway."

""Huh?"" they asked in unison, as if trying to say, *What are you talking about?*

"Um, but he can fly, y'know?"

"Won't he be long gone by the time we get out of this manhole...?"

"But why would we need to go the roundabout way? If he can fly, so will I."

""Huh?"" They stared at me, bug-eyed.

I cast *Skywalker*, the spell for flight, letting my body gently float in the air.

"B-but I thought humans couldn't fly...?!"

"Is that so? Well, I can. Remember that for next time," I told the flabbergasted duo. "I'm off now."

With that, I began to soar, continuing through the gaping shaft upward to pursue my target. I spotted him near the opening up top, and right before he was about to emerge from the ground, I halted his movements by casting an elementary attack spell, *Flare*. The flames blasted straight toward the beast.

"*Graaaaaaaaaaaah?!*" he hollered as he was engulfed in fire, but he was apparently tougher than he'd let on.

I'd initially planned on making him crash from the force of the explosion, but that didn't exactly pan out...and somehow let him escape aboveground instead.

"*Ngaaaaaaaaah!*"

As soon as we emerged from the hole, the demon yanked a girl within arm's reach by the base of her neck, thrusting her in front of him as if she were a shield. All the while, he remained silent, which I assumed was because he was in too much pain to muster the energy to speak, but he still managed to make his intentions clear.

That said, the real problem wasn't him taking a hostage: It was the fact that we'd surfaced on a main road. This was the worst-case scenario for sure. I mean, the never-ending stream of pedestrians was now totally fixated on this sudden intruder who'd appeared from the depths of the earth.

Even with the enemy completely covered with burn wounds, people could still easily tell that he was a demon.

"H-hey, is that...?!"

Fear spread among the masses.

"*Ahhhhhhhhhh?!*"

"*R-run away! It's the demooooons!*"

Mayhem ensued.

This is bad. This is really bad. Something had to be done quickly or pandemonium would break out and maybe even spark a riot.

...I really don't want to do this, but I guess I have no choice.

I took a deep breath—and shouted to the crowd raising hell in their efforts to escape.

"*Listen up, everyone! My name is Ard Meteor! The son of the Great Mages!*" I boomed, cutting through the screams and panic.

The place became so silent that it was almost as if there was never any commotion to begin with.

"Th-the son of the Great Mages...?!"

"C-come to think of it, there were rumors that he'd entered the academy this year..."

I really hadn't wanted to stand out, but there was nothing else I could have done. To calm the people, I'd chosen to stand front and center.

"I've been secretly chasing down that demon over there to the brink of death! And now, I will extinguish that which threatens the lives of good people! For I—the son of the Great Mages—will rain divine punishment down on him!"

What an embarrassing speech, I thought to myself as I glared at the demon who was the source of my troubles.

As I began to construct a certain spell in my head, he shot me a little grin, apparently having recovered enough to talk.

He mocked, "You, defeat *me*? You fool! Don't you see I have a hostage—?"

"A hostage? I don't see any hostage."

"Ha! She's right…over…h-here…?!" he stuttered as his eyes popped out of his head.

The girl who had just been shielding him was nowhere to be seen.

"When did you start hallucinating that there was a hostage?"

"Y-you bastard! What did you do?!"

"Just a bit of an illusion spell. I saved the girl after casting it. It's not very effective against those who are mentally strong, but, like, I guess the quality of demons has gone down in recent years."

"Dammit…! Dammit all to heeeell! What in the world are you?!!"

As I let out a heavy sigh, I finished composing my attack spell.

"I'm your average villager. What about it?"

"And you expect me to believe that?!" he screeched with tears brimming in his eyes as he beat his wings and soared into the sky. This guy really didn't know when to quit.

"You don't seem to get it. Allow me to enlighten you," I declared, pointing a finger at the flying demon. "(Demon) Lord knows, you'll never escape."

With that, I cast my spell, unleashing an enormous magic circle in his direction, and it gradually began to rotate, floating in the empty space between us.

"*Flash of Babel*, fire," I chanted, unleashing a flood of golden light that quickly sought out and washed over its target in an instant.

But it didn't stop there. The destructive beam of light shot upward into the sky, puncturing a ginormous hole among the clouds, where it finally reached its zenith and died out. I bet that demon had fallen onto some street in a charred heap—but he shouldn't be dead or anything. I made sure of that. Taking that weakling's life wouldn't do me any good. Plus, he still needed to cough up some answers.

All settled, or so I'd thought.

"Th-that thing just now...!"

"I-I've seen it before! That was the spell of the Great Mages! The most powerful and advanced magic on earth!"

"Th-then that brat over there... I mean, that young man must be—!"

...Ah, this is just what I expected would happen, I thought as the crowd surrounded me and began to cause a stir.

"Ah, of course, the son of our great heroes!"

"Thank you for saving us!"

"We're so grateful...so grateful...!"

The people in the streets were hoisting me high into the air before I had a chance put an end to this madness.

...Why did it come to this?!

As I continued to float up and down, I let out a deeply, deeply agonized sigh.

...Fast-forward. I had pinpointed the demon's whereabouts based on his trail of magical residue and tracked him down, but when I reached his location, he'd already taken his own life, apparently using a spell that erased every last trace of his spirit and soul.

Thanks for nothing. This meant I couldn't resurrect him to get more information.

And the ones in the sewer were in the exact same condition.

I hated to admit this about our enemy, but they'd really thought through this plan and earned some of my respect. On the other hand, this whole situation was confusing and frightening enough to make me restless.

What in the world do they want? I hadn't the slightest idea.

Given that they were demons, there was a pretty big chance they wanted to retaliate against Ireena's and my parents, the Great Mages and the Heroic Baron…but this theory didn't explain their plan to kidnap us.

At any rate, I better take more precautions from now on.

Incidentally, the little affair of defeating the demon was totally blown out of proportion by the public, even though it didn't seem like a particularly big deal to me. I mean, there was even a knightly looking man calling himself an emissary of the queen who came to inform us that Her Majesty would honor us with an audience and requested that the two of us visit her at the palace.

I'd preferred to avoid garnering any more attention…but this recent development was more than I'd imagined for myself. If I could get the queen to agree to join me at the negotiating table, I'd be able to decline the battle event—you know, the one that'd been plaguing me. That was exactly why I headed toward the palace at the heart of the royal capital. I was grasping tightly onto this one wish.

The interior and exterior of the castle were every bit as magnificent and resplendent as you'd imagine for a royal home in the very heart of the nation. That said, it really wasn't practical at all. Back in my heyday, I'd lived in the Castle Millennion, which had been built from 103,000 types of magical techniques, making it impervious to outside attacks and capable of unleashing special-class offensive spells.

If you compare this castle to that one, the queen's was unreliable at best. I mean, if this structure were in the old world, it'd be blasted away without a trace.

I guess this all means there's peace on earth and no need to fret over these small things, I thought as I tailed after our knightly guide through the palace.

…I'd totally assumed our meeting would be super informal and take place in the guest parlor, but I was proven wrong when we were led to a large reception hall.

In other words, it wasn't a casual affair at all but a true audience—meaning official business. Men and women, young and old, who I assumed were vassals stiffly lined the walls, eyeing me up and down and chattering among themselves: "What's this bratty commoner doing in the palace…?" or "I propose we execute these Great Mages. Any old reason will do."

All their comments stressed their hatred toward peasants like me, which made for the most unwarm welcome.

Beside Ireena, I prostrated myself as we waited for the queen's entrance, staring at the long carpet spread out underneath me leading to a magnificent throne… Even though I was gazing upon it as a commoner, I wasn't particularly moved by it or anything. In fact, all I felt was pity for the person who had to sit there.

And then the queen herself, Rosa, made her grand appearance.

From the other end of the aisle, Her Majesty the Queen was surrounded by some burly knights.

Her beauty and prestige stood at the pinnacle of the modern world.

I'm guessing she wasn't that much older than us—one or two years, tops—and neither too tall nor too short. She had a long and slender frame that didn't possess particularly big boobs, unlike Ireena…but her body was absolutely stunning, wrapped in a golden dress hugging every inch. True, her breasts might be modest in size compared to Ireena and

Ginny, but it was as if they were artfully shaped, and her curvaceous hips traced an arc that cut through the air.

In all honesty, words were too limited to express the extent of her perfection. She possessed a mature sort of beauty that was worthy of the regal appearance of a monarch.

That said...I was way more concerned about that hair—blond locks twisted into tight coils.

How in the world does she get them to stay like that? This had bothered me in my previous life, and it was still a mystery—

"Hey, commoner! You have no right to look directly upon Her Majesty's noble countenance!" barked an old man behind Rosa.

He had a handlebar mustache and trailed the queen with sprightly movements. I guessed he was the prime minister.

Queen Rosa took her seat on her throne. "All is well. For it's nature's wish that all living creatures are captivated by my beauty," she stated, waving a luxurious fan in front of her smile.

There was no arrogance in her voice—only supreme confidence in herself.

Well, how should I go about this? How exactly does one deal with the queen? I wondered.

"Rosie! It's been too long! How've ya been?!" Ireena asked, snapping up from the ground with a huge grin.

It'd been a while since I'd felt the blood drain out of my face. If she treated the queen that way—

"What's with this girl?!"

"How dare she insult Her Majesty...!"

"It doesn't matter if she's the daughter of the Heroic Baron or not! This is a grave offense!"

These reactions came as no surprise, and the danger pervading the room jumped up by 70 percent.

But even with this major shift, Ireena grandly puffed out her chest.

"What's your problem?! I'm not hurting anybody, right?! Besides, we're friends!" she shouted back, to which all the nobles grimaced.

As for the queen, she shook with mirth. "Goodness, you ne'er change. This is thy true self, the Ireena I know," she said, chuckling with merriment.

With that, her eyes swept across the nobles in the room, and she reprimanded them sternly. "Ireena is a friend of mine, and thus any and all forwardness is permitted. If you have any complaints, speak to me directly. I will not tolerate any untoward remarks directed at her."

Her intimidating shift in tone silenced everyone in the room.

I couldn't believe it. The queen was her friend. My Ireena was a superstar.

Rosa smiled elegantly and snapped open her fan. "Ah, yes. I've called thee here today for one reason: to praise thee for the remarkable achievement of defeating a demon by thyself. And to bestow a reward. That is, unto you, Ard Meteor."

Her eyes pierced straight into mine.

...*Well, what do I do now?*

I'd dealt with foreign royals more than I could count. But that was all back when I was the Demon Lord. This was my first time having an audience with one as a low-class human.

So how exactly does a commoner address a queen?

Come on—you gotta remember. How did your subordinates and citizens act toward you?

...*Oh right, that's it: They always answered everything I said with "yes!" Yeah, now I remember. It was always "yes!" "yes!" "yes!"*

And by *everything*, I meant it. Especially some of the villagers: They'd earnestly reply with "yes!" even if I'd asked, "Do you hate me?"

...When I heard that, I'd honestly considered ramping up their annual tribute by one hundred times.

Well, anyway. Until we got to the negotiation table, my new plan was to answer everything with "yes!"

"Thy actions have done us a great service."

"Yes!"

"And they're worthy of great merit."

"Yes!"

"As expected of the son of the Great Mages."

"Yes!"

"I have taken a great interest in thee and shall gift thee with a reward."

"Yes!"

"Become my husband."

"Ye— I mean, what?!"

She'd dropped a bomb with this request, leaving me absolutely dumbfounded—along with everyone else in the room.

"Hmm? Is it so beyond thy comprehension? Allow me to repeat myself in simpler terms: Ard Meteor, impregnate me, won't you?" asked Her Majesty the Queen, smiling sweetly upon me and moving her thighs slowly to cross her legs.

She licked her lips in a way that was super erotic...and even managed to make my heart pound, even though I thought I'd gotten used to seeing beautiful women by now. But that moment was over in a matter of an instant, and the booming wrath of those around her brought me back to my senses.

"H-has she gone mad?!"

"It'd be unacceptable to have a filthy commoner's blood mix with the queen's!"

"This is why I'd proposed we completely purge all of the lower class!"

The vassals went berserk, with the prime minister taking center stage.

"Your Majesty! What could you possibly see in this ruuuuube?! Unacceptable! I oppose your decision with every fiber of my being! Why

this commoner...? Ah! I see! So *that's* what you've been craving. In that case, no need to worry! I'll gladly serve as your nightly companion, Your Majesty! No worries whatsoever! My naughty serviceman is a *grade-A stud*! I bring the *big* guns, unlike that brat! Seriously!"

"Heeey, yo. Could someone pleeeease slit this dirty old lolicon's throat?"

But even as the prime minister continued to rant and rave, Queen Rosa completely ignored him and carried on with business.

"My word, it can be so restricting to be a queen. Ah well. Let's just say this was a playful jest and leave it at that," she concluded, slumping her shoulders forward and shaking her head vigorously from side to side.

In all honesty, it didn't seem like her eyes held even the smallest crumb of affection for me. There was some other emotion I could sense... But Rosa started to talk before I could guess what it might possibly be.

"I must admit, I have other matters to deal with. Let's wrap this up. For your reward, Ard Meteor, I bestow thee with the title of Pentagon, a promotion to the fifth rank of the magic arts," she mentioned brusquely.

And the room fell into an uproar at the mind-boggling news once again.

"A-a Pentagon?! N-no commoner has ever been made a Pentagon before!"

"It's one thing for a child prodigy from an aristocratic family like Elrado! But for a peasant? This is too much!"

"Your Majesty! Please do not continue any further! I'm certain this will inflate the grandiosity of the masses if you grant this promotion to a non-noble! It might even become grounds for an insurrection!"

I thought that last claim was a little far-fetched. At any rate, it wasn't like I wanted to be a Pentagon! Like, not in the slightest! I could already see a huge smile spreading across Olivia's face at the news. This was the number one thing I absolutely needed to avoid, so I chose my next words carefully.

"My deepest apologies, Your Majesty, but I must admit your vassals are right that this title is much too great for a simple commoner. I am aware that this may come across as disrespectful…but I hope you might grant my modest wish as a reward."

"Oh? And what might your request be? Pray tell."

I smirked internally at this opportunity. "I wish for you to increase the federal budget of my school, the Laville National Academy of Magic."

If this went through, there'd be no reason for me to participate in the battle event.

Queen Rosa cocked her head to the side, eyes wide at my request. "What? Is that it? Really? And how will that benefit you?"

"No personal benefit. But the headmaster, Count Golde, has done so much for me on a day-to-day basis, and this is the least I could do to repay some of his kindness…"

Finally, the vassals started to take on an air of compassion.

"Ah, the commoner knows his place."

"The complete opposite of his parents. If that's the case, I suppose there's no need to interfere."

"We could grant him the title of Triangle and promote him to the third rank. That should be harmless enough. There's no doubt of his excellence, and I'm sure we can expect him to do good work."

Nice! Turning threats into support with one fell swoop—

"What virtue! To prioritize repaying a debt over thy desire! I have never met one like thee! I'm intrigued by thee, Ard Meteor! As a reward, I will make thee a Pentagon *and* increase the budget!"

…Thanks to the queen's idiocy, the vassals took up their hostile

tone once again. After even more back and forth, she finally managed
to get a grip on the whole situation.

"Agh! Enough! Enough! Fine, I get it! What if I add a condition
to this reward? Ard Meteor and Ireena Litz de Olhyde, in exchange
for granting you both the title of Pentagon, I will include you in my
personal guard who report directly to me, the Queen's Shadow. I will
regularly send you out on challenging quests."

"...I'm sorry, Your Majesty. Er, we have more points of contention
now. Bestowing the daughter of Olhyde with the title of Pentagon is—"

"I see no issue. Think of it as a bonus. I assume she'll reach that
level someday. Plus, it'd look bad if her partner is a Pentagon while
she's stuck in the first rank, a Single. Don't you agree, Ireena?"

"Right on! That's my Rosie! As thoughtful as ever!" Ireena chirped
back happily.

The queen smiled in satisfaction upon seeing joy spread across
Ireena's face.

Of course, there was a whole mess and then some afterward, as I'd
expected.

With the queen's concluding words ("All righty! That settles it!
Duty calls! I don't wanna hear any more of this! Good-bye! Adios!"),
we were locked into our new titles and enlistment in the mysterious
group known as the Queen's Shadow.

"Dammit! I still don't know how to wrangle in the current queen!"

"Come now, try to calm down. Let's have a nice long chat about
that commoner. There's no problem at all. If we take advantage of the
fact they're in the Queen's Shadow..."

"Indeed. We can go about this in any number of ways... Let them
bask in their new status. For now."

...Geez, the politicians of this era really need to take other people's
feelings into consideration.

"Wowie, what unexpected news! Let's write our parents when

we get back! Ah, I can already see Daddy just exploding over the news!"

Sure. But I think he'll be "exploding" in another way.

The issue of the battle event might have been settled for the time being, but now I'd been roped into joining the Queen's Shadow or whatever, and a completely new problem had dropped into my lap.

Seriously, why do things keep turning out like this?

The sun was slowly dipping beneath the horizon at the royal capital.

In the center of a deserted back alley, a number of men and women had gathered, appearing upon first glance to be nothing more than your average commoners.

In actuality, they were part of a crime syndicate run by demons known as Lars al Ghoul.

An elderly one who looked like the leader among them spoke in a strong, clear voice. "That son of the Great Mages is more skilled than expected."

But his little speech held an unexpectedly peppy tone, and the others around the old demon nodded with pleasant expressions.

"Aye. I was able to take measure of his power during the recent incident."

"We had to sacrifice some of our kin…but our grief will be completely washed away with this."

"Right. That Ard Meteor is certainly a strong one. Clearly beyond the norm. But…he cannot win against *that monster.*"

In their mind's eye, everyone conjured the image of *her,* their collaborator. Their faces were colored by two emotions—relief…and distrust.

"Can we really trust that woman? She's a different species

from us, after all. Isn't she known throughout history as a famous traitor?"

But the elderly demon was confident. "I understand your misgivings, but there is no cause for concern. She will not betray us because her devotion is genuine. She's quite keen on destroying this world. And that's why we're using her." He broke out into a wicked smile.

"Sure, she does hate *that* world, but she's far too strong. Once our master returns for their second coming, we'll need to get rid of her somehow, lest she ruins that reign, too," someone continued matter-of-factly.

The old demon changed the subject. "Well, no changes to this current matter. We'll need to *abduct our sacrifice* on the day the stars are aligned. That is, seven days from now. We won't perform the *ceremony* until then. Take your time carrying away the sacrifice, and don't act in haste or of your own accord. The enemy could catch on to our plan with one wrong move. If that happens, we might find ourselves in the worst-case scenario. We can count the most powerful monster as our ally, but don't let that be the reason you lower your guard."

The group nodded as one.

The leader continued. "No changes to the details of the plan, either. Thanks to this recent incident, we now know the extent of Ard Meteor's power. He's unneeded in this world. There's no call for a complex plan: It'll all come down to brute force. Employ all our forces to kidnap the sacrifice. That's it. In the past, we might have incorporated suicide missions, but we now command limitless power and that fearsome beast is on our side," he boomed with effusive optimism, bringing his speech to a close. "Everything we do is to bring the world under our master's command and resurrect true morality."

"*All Hail Outer.*" Following their leader's chant, each of the members murmured this in turn…and then scattered separately back into the milling crowds. Once he was alone, the elderly demon walked toward the main road, where he overheard a conversation among the townspeople.

"It's in *seven more days*, huh."

"I can't wait for *the battle event at the academy* this year."

"Right? I mean, after all, the kids of *those great heroes* just enrolled at the school."

As he listened in on this conversation, the elderly demon muttered to himself, "Yes, what fun indeed," and his wrinkly face twisted hideously.

CHAPTER 15
The Ex–Demon Lord and Girl Trouble, Part I

I'd been enlisted into the Queen's Shadow and promoted to the title of Pentagon, which were two secrets I guarded with my life. Or so I'd thought until a certain trick of fate—or the schemes of a select few aristocrats—caused word to get out and spread like wildfire.

Thanks to all that, everyone started to treat me differently at the academy. The noble students stopped openly despising me. Then, there was the creation of the Lord Ard Fan Club, which meant that a gaggle of commoner girls would follow me around every which way I went.

Oh, and…a new girl would confess to me every day without fail.

The lukewarm wind of early summer stroked my cheek as we stood in the shadows of the academic building after school. A girl in the same grade as me gazed into my eyes with a flushed face, fidgeting shyly and hesitating until she sucked in a deep breath as if she'd finally made up her mind.

"I—I like you! Please go out with me!" she shouted, bowing her head earnestly and thrusting out her right hand for me to take if I accepted.

The first time it happened, my heart felt like it would leap out of my chest, but I'd gotten used to it by this point. In all honesty, I didn't feel much when I delivered my usual line.

"I'm sorry. I have too much going on right now to even think about love. I can't go out with you at the moment, but let's start off as friends."

There was a boatload of girls with varying levels of attractiveness who'd confessed to me...plus a few guys, but let's not get into the nitty-gritty, since the most important takeaway was that I couldn't get romantically involved with anyone. A player might have fooled around, but I couldn't do something so dishonest.

"...It's okay—I understand. I'm sorry for getting all weird on you," she apologized, clearly heartbroken, though she seemed to take my response rather well.

I could see that she couldn't hide her look of shock before she hung her head, softly trembling. I still had no idea what to do in these—

"...Keeping me as another side chick, huh. How can I get him to fall for me?"

Huh?

"He screams *virgin*. Doesn't he seem the type to cave with one sultry look?"

Hold it.

"I could let him feel up my tits. One thing might lead to another and it's possible he'd knock me up, and next thing you know, his family fortune would be all mine...! Heh-heh-heh, then I'd be filthy stinkin' rich...!"

Hey. I can hear you—and your evil side.

"A-all right, Ard... Now that we're friends, I want to ask you for a favor... Can you fondle my boobs?"

"I'm afraid not..."

"Huh?! Why?!"

Why are you so surprised? If anyone should be shocked, it was me. There was no way I could just grope them.

"But, Ard, um, er, you seem so tired."

What does that have to do with boobs? Was she suggesting it would get rid of my fatigue? There was no way... Okay, well, I take that back. Maybe Ireena's could manage to do that.

But the girl in front of me would have no such effect, which meant I absolutely refused.

"Um, well... *C'mon and grab my boobs alreadyyyyyy!*" she yelled, finally resorting to pure force.

What's with this girl? She was absolutely terrifying, trying to yank my arms toward her to make me grope her breasts, but I wasn't about to let her, sprinting with everything I had. *What the hell is this?*

"*Mwa-ha-ha-ha-ha! Feel me uppppp! Feel me up goooood!*"

She was a true monster—far scarier than any spirits or demons I'd fought against in the past. Oh, if this was the old world, I could just scream "*Come on, you lot! Attaaaaaaaaack!*" and that'd be enough to finish the job. But as a mere villager, I had no backup, obviously.

No, really, I'm serious. Someone help me, I thought...and the heavens must have heard my prayers, for a familiar voice cut through the beastly howls that very next moment.

"This has gone far enough!" someone barked, full of rage.

It was...Ireena, standing imposingly by the corner of the school with her arms crossed, emanating a fierce demonic aura. Even as the ex–Demon Lord, I broke out in a cold sweat.

The monster (er, that girl from earlier) must have clearly felt Ireena's wrath, as she stopped dead in her tracks, sweating profusely.

"U-um, that's, uh......... *Boobies! Boobies!*" she finally spouted before she ran away.

"Y-you saved me... Thank you, Ireena..."

I walked toward her, fully expecting her to break out in a smile and say something along the lines of *Heh-heh-heh! I'm amazing!* I called it her "praise me, master!" vibes.

But she left me with an unhappy "hmph!" and turned to the

side, averting her eyes as she walked away without another word. I'd noticed only recently, but I had surmised that Ireena was the jealous type.

That said, I wasn't stupid. You see, her actions would have a lot of inexperienced men think, *That girl has the hots for me!* But I knew better than that. She was thinking something like, *He's my friend and mine alone. I don't want anyone to take him away from me.* Yeah, it wasn't like she liked me in that way in the slightest.

I understood her feelings. I felt the same way: I wanted to eradicate every last insect that crawled near her with impure intentions. Huh. I could do it now. In fact, that's what I was gonna be doing.

…Anyhow, it seemed Ireena had been in a bad mood with me lately. And seeing as her smile was my fuel, this was a matter of life and death. I had to settle the matter quickly…but it wouldn't be easy.

"Oh, it's so hard to navigate relationships…," I mused as the tepid wind enveloped me in the shadows of the academic building, where I drew a long breath and let out a heavy sigh.

…I'd returned to my dorm, where I had dinner as usual and rinsed off my sweat in the communal bath before lolling in my bed.

"Phew… Now, what to do? I'll do anything to cheer her up."

Nothing came to mind. I knew that the root of the issue was all these girls confessing to me, but I couldn't come up with a single solution to this problem. If all I wanted to do was stop them from falling in love with me, I could stand on the rooftop in broad daylight and shout at the top of my lungs, *I LIKE BOOOOOOOOOOOYS!* to strike 'em out all at once. But then my life would be over. And my relationship with Ireena.

"Hrmmmmm. If one of the Council of Seven were here, I bet they'd impart some wisdom."

I rolled around the bed as the gears turned in my mind.

Knock, knock. The sound echoed inside the room.

…Is it Ireena? Is she here to patch things up? I wondered, holding on to wishful thinking as I granted entry.

The door swung open to reveal a certain someone—

"Hee-hee-hee… I thought I'd drop on by. ♪"

It wasn't Ireena but Ginny, wrapped in a heavy, long coat even though it was almost summertime. *But why?* I wondered, cocking my head to the side.

Whoosh. Ginny opened her long coat and flung it off.

And her exposed body…was wrapped in crimson string. Well, it'd be more accurate to say it was wrapped in nothing but said thread. It was one thin cord stretching from her groin to her chest, passing across her shoulders, and that was it.

Meaning she was pretty much naked.

With her stark white and velvety skin, enormous boobs, and a butt I couldn't help but want to squeeze, all of Ginny's unique and fiendish arsenal was on full display.

"What do you think? My mother said I looked great, but…"

"E-even if you ask me that, I…"

"Okay, different question… Do I make you excited?"

I couldn't give a direct answer. It was too embarrassing.

Her face lit up with a sweet smile, as if she'd read my thoughts.

"If I said you could have your way with me, what would you do?"

"Huh? No, well, uh… What do you mean?" I replied with a question of my own, which drew a troubled, lamented sigh from Ginny.

"Ard, you've been popular with the girls, especially as of late. And that's perfectly fine. I've said this for a while now, but I really am pushing for this harem agenda of mine. That said… I wouldn't want someone other than me to be your number one. That's why…," she trailed off, tilting her head to swish her peach hair and flashing a seductive smirk. "I thought I'd turn the heat up a notch."

And with that, Ginny closed in on me. This was the part where I needed to stop her or flee from the scene. But my body was locked in place. *No way. Is this…?*

"Ard, I can tell you want to do it, too. I can see it in your eyes," she noted, her breasts swaying from side to side as she drew near…

The closer she got, the more I noticed new additions appearing on Ginny's body. When I saw that a glossy black tail had snaked out of her butt, I was certain: This girl had just awakened as a high-ranking succubus.

All succubi have a species-specific skill known as *Charm*, with the more powerful ones possessing an advanced version called *Charming Evil Eye*. It was one of the three great Evil Eyes, giving its wielder the ability to control the heart and agency of anyone by locking eyes with their target. Her horns, tail, and hearts in her eyes were all proof that she held its power.

This was bad. It'd be a different story back in my heyday, but this body of mine was perfectly average for ancient times.

And I needed that technique to fend off the *Charming Evil Eye*…!

…Before I'd realized it, Ginny was right by my side, sliding her hands on my shoulders.

"It's my first time, too…but don't worry. I'll make you feel real good, ♡" she breathed into my ear, pinning me down on the bed.

Th-this was real bad. I couldn't move. And what's more, I was accepting this situation.

I couldn't help but think from the bottom of my heart that I wanted to do all sorts of things with Ginny. I'd managed to hold back any physiological responses by a hairbreadth.

"First, we'll make you nice and big. ♪"

It was only a matter of time. Am I gonna ascend the stairs to adulthood? I thought, just when the face of a certain other girl flashed in my mind.

The following events must have been a trick of fate.

"A-Ard! I'm comin' in, okay...?" That very same girl opened the door and entered.

Yep, I'm talking about Ireena, who immediately turned to stone upon seeing Ginny in her birthday suit, reaching for my nether regions, and me, pinned down and red-faced.

...I know it's getting old by now. But let me just say it again.

Why do things turn out this way?!

CHAPTER 16
The Ex–Demon Lord and Girl Trouble, Part II

"Wh-wh-wh-wh-wh-wh-wha...?!" Ireena sputtered, eyes agape at our madness as her entire body quivered. Her face was flushed bright red.

For an inexplicable reason, her outfit was also extreme: She was in a white bikini top with a blue miniskirt—so short that her black thong was easily visible.

Why is she dressed like that? I wondered... But that was clearly a question for another time, since I needed to devote my full attention to something else entirely.

"*What do you think you're doiiiiiing?!*"

How can I deescalate her explosive rage? I thought as Ireena let out a mighty roar and closed the distance between us, her silver hair trailing after her in a blur as she tackled Ginny and ripped her off me.

"*Stupid! Stupid, stupid, stupid, stupid! Ard, you're so stupid!*" she shrieked, riding on top of me in place of Ginny and pummeling her fists into my face.

The sweet objections of a young maiden? Yeah, right. This was way too punishing for that. She continued to strike me from a mounted position with enough force to make a martial arts master go pale. Her punches freakin' hurt.

"Gwah! Uwagh! Argh! I-Ireena, please calm… Blargh?!"

"Uwaaaaaaaaagh! Ard, you *stupid dummyyyyyyy!*" Ireena cried as a fountain of tears poured from her blue eyes.

Ginny approached this spectacle from behind. "How uncouth. You know, this is gonna make him hate you."

With that, Ireena's entire body shuddered, and her fists stopped in midair—which Ginny grabbed, pinning her arms behind her back and tearing her away from me.

Then Ginny fixed her eyes on Ireena. "Think back, Miss Ireena. What are you here to do in the first place?"

"I—I came…because I wanted to make up with Ard… I've been really mean to him lately… But I didn't want him to not like me anymore…," Ireena trailed off uncomfortably.

"Ohhh? I seeee… And I'm assuming this outfit of yours is part of your little plan to make up?"

"Y-yeah! It's all because his mom, Carla, told me that b-boys will do anything if you wear s-s-s-s-sexy clothing!"

…*Oh, Mother. What have you been indoctrinating my precious girl with?*

"And then, um… I think she said that we'd both feel really good and make up if we did something… I think it started with the letter *S*! And so I'm here to do that thing with Ard!"

…*I'll have to chat with my mother sometime soon.*

"I see, I see… By the way, Miss Ireena, how do you do that 'thing'?"

"Th-that's, uh… A-Ard will teach me!"

"…Pfft (lol)!"

"Wha—?! What's so funny?!"

"Oh, nothing. I was just thinking that your childish naïveté makes you so charming. That's all. I mean, you're how old? And you don't know anything about this? Really? You're so innocent!"

"Grrr…! Listen up! I know you're making fun of me! First off! This all happened because you made moves on Ard! Ever since you got super-cozy with him, I can't even sit still! I've been able to bear it up until this point! But now! It makes my blood boil to see these girls around him!"

"Yikes. As a lady, I can't believe you're blaming your shortcomings on others."

"A lady? What about you is ladylike?! Y-you're wearing th-th-th-that o-obscene outfit!"

Sparks flew between the two girls.

Ireena was flushed red with anger, staring daggers with her eyes. "Fine! Let's settle this with a duel! I'll wipe the floor with you at the battle event!"

"Ooooh, you're sooo wild! …Then again, I guess I'm sometimes a little wild, too," Ginny admitted with a fierce look in her eyes. "Okay. I accept your challenge. I mean, I'm gonna win anyway."

"You sure talk big…! In that case, swear you'll never go near Ard again if you lose!"

"Fine, fine, I promise. To sweeten the deal, I'll even offer to do a lap around the capital—buck naked. But if you lose, you gotta do it, too."

"Bring it on! I'll do a hundred laps without a shred of clothing! And I'll eat a meat pie through my nose!"

Their hair bristled as they declared war on each other. I would joke, *What troubled times!* but it clearly wasn't the time or the place for that. I guess I was so worried that I was about to engage in some serious escapism.

But I couldn't bear the idea of seeing these two hurt each other, so I squashed down my anxieties and fears.

"P-please calm down, both of you!"

Two sets of eyes glared at me at once. The pressure was mounting, and this was honestly scarier than fighting some of the "champions" out there. But I couldn't back down now.

To establish some semblance of hierarchy between us, I held back the serious urge to grovel and mustered up my courage.

"You two! Sit on your heels, now!" I barked, trying my best to look as ticked off as possible.

It apparently worked, as a shiver ran down their bodies like they were scolded puppies. Their anger seemed to dissolve out of them completely, replaced with fear, as they sat down before me.

"What's this business about a duel?! Nothing about this is grounds to hurt or hate each other! I absolutely forbid you from dueling! Apologize to each other and make up! Otherwise, no food for you!" I commanded, feeling like a pet owner all the while.

The two mumbled a bit but raised no objections and turned toward each other.

"I-I'm sorry for snapping at you, Ginny."

"I—I apologize as well. I got carried away and went too far."

The two shook hands, remaining seated on the ground as they apologized to each other. *I knew these two were good, honest kids at heart.* This was why I liked them.

Now that this is settled...

"I heard everything!"

A trespasser flamboyantly kicked down the door into the room, and our eyes all turned at once to see a platinum blonde with locks that reached all the way down to the floor. With delicate and dollish features, the intruder was none other than our teacher Jessica.

Her hands planted on her hips as she flashed us a grin, thrusting out her big chest. "If you can't have a duel, have at it during the battle event."

...I had a bad feeling about this. I began to sweat as I let the situation reach its natural conclusion.

"But Ard won't be in it," Ireena objected.

"If he's not gonna participate, I have no desire to do so, either."

"All right, I get that you're not all for it. But be the tiniest bit flexible and participate in the event," Jessica urged, pausing for a brief moment before delivering her final line, which went far beyond my wildest imagination: "It's part of Operation: Instructor Ard."

After a few moments of muted shock, I managed to find my voice, trembling with disbelief. "Wha—?! Wh-what are you talking about?!"

"Can't you tell by the name? The role of a student isn't enough for you, meaning you should become an instructor... That's what the headmaster said."

What the hell, ya old geezer?

"That said...we're facing a lot of opposition, particularly with the aristocratic instructors. They're all saying there's no way they'd ever recognize a commoner child as a fellow teacher, and they won't even try to listen to us."

Great job, guys. Keep it up.

"But we'll be able to win them over if we have suitable achievements. This is where the battle event comes in. Ard has personally trained the two of you. If you win, it'll be proof of his prowess as a teacher and give us the opening this operation needs."

Ginny and Ireena nodded in complete agreement.

"With all that said, will you two join the event?" she appealed to the girls, who were looking like they were seriously mulling this over.

This isn't good. Not good at all. Operation: Instructor Ard? There was no way I could let that happen. If I became an instructor, I'd end up spending even more time around Olivia. Meaning I'd see her dazzling smile all the damn time. That was the last thing I wanted, so I figured I'd give these two a stern warning.

"I've mentioned this time and time again: Magic exists to help those in need or to stay true to your principles, not to flaunt your power before the masses. The battle event directly opposes these beliefs, which is why—"

Ireena and Ginny assumed very serious expressions.

Excellent. This obnoxious operation is as good as done. Wow, these two are honest, upright—

"…Hey, you two. Don't you want to see Ard looking all cool in the instructor's uniform?" Jessica piped up.

""I do!"" they replied.

…Yep, honest, upright girls… Greediness and all.

"No, um, I never agreed to—"

"If I'm gonna participate, I'm definitely gonna win!"

"Wait just a—"

"Heh-heh-heh. I won't lose to you, Miss Ireena."

"I'm telling you, my—"

""I'll fight you head-on!"" they shouted, shaking on it as heated rivals and trailing after Jessica to leave the room.

It was like I wasn't even there.

…Oh geez, I could really use a good cry or two.

"Ha-ha-ha. I guess popular boys have it rough, eh?" Jessica gave me a few hearty slaps on my back with a cheerful look. "Oh, the battle event can't come soon enough. And I mean it," she murmured, keeping her usual smile plastered on her face.

It must be my imagination.

But for some reason, I could swear there was something wicked lurking under her grin.

CHAPTER 17
The Ex–Demon Lord, a Battle
Event, and Absolute Mayhem

During the seven days leading up to the battle event, I tried my hand at any and all forms of sabotage, but fate was a cruel mistress. Every single plan somehow managed to fail in ways that went far beyond any reasonable possibility, and the day of the battle event arrived without a hitch.

Why do things turn out like this?

It was staged at the largest multipurpose stadium in the royal castle, which was a coliseum from ancient times that'd been renovated and expanded to comfortably house twenty thousand people. And since the Laville National Academy of Magic was praised across the entire continent, its annual battle event was hugely popular...and resulted in a packed stadium.

As sunlight filled the open arena and the guests roared with ear-splitting cheers at the flashy one-on-one battles, the energy of the spectators was reaching a fever pitch. One of the primary causes was our students engaging in hardcore fights, and the other was...the fact that Ireena's father and my parents—in other words, the Heroic Baron and the Great Mages—were acting as special guest MCs for the event.

I'm sorry. Were you expecting to hear some high-level commentary from true heroes?

"These one-on-ones between the girls aren't really doing it for me. Throw in a gal who looks like a gorilla or something, and that's sure to shake things up."

"It might not be enough for you, but we've definitely got some lookers here! Their boobs are just the perfect size, and they have the cutest tushies. I think I'll go say hi when this is all over. *Slurp.*"

Well, my parents stopped being decent humans a long time ago, and I hate to tell you that your hopes are wasted.

"There are a few attack spells by Lemming that have come as complete surprises, but Lizzie is wonderfully perceptive. You can't forget that common sense is just as important as magical prowess on the battlefield, which means we still can't tell how this battle will play out," announced Weiss, who was actually giving commentary that was concise and easy for the masses to understand, unlike my stupid parents.

As expected of Weiss. After all, he ranked number one on my list of People Who I Wish Were My Father.

I was right behind our special guests, perched in a front row box seat to watch over the proceedings. There was someone right next to me.

"This is some match. Don't you think they're both talented?"

"I agree," I said to Olivia, who was sitting one seat over from me with a fantastic smile plastered across her face.

I refused to let mine fade, either, which was why some weird rumors were floating around.

"They have serious chemistry…"

"I guess they really are an item."

Most of them were a *huge* misunderstanding.

There was no way in hell we had any kind of chemistry. This was far from a pleasant conversation between opposite sexes: It was a high-stakes battle of mental fortitude.

"Wow, some top-notch students. I'd be willing to bet even Alvarto would make the two of them his apprentices. Don't you agree?"

"Well, I've never had the pleasure of meeting Sir Alvarto, so I'm afraid I cannot say."

Olivia had been spouting nonsense for a while now and sizing up my reactions. I'd be done for if I slipped up by assuming even a fraction of a micro-expression like *nah, no way*. She had the ability to perceive her opponent's thoughts through the smallest facial changes, which meant I had to maintain a cool smile and frantically suppress the urge to make any snarky comments.

But wow. That'd been a close one. There was no way that the most war-crazed of the Four Heavenly Kings would ever take any apprentices. I mean, he was the type of guy to actively hound talent and leave them in a condition beyond all recovery. Alvarto killed anyone the moment he realized their potential.

...I wonder what he's up to these days, I pondered, continuing to observe the event without dropping my guard against Olivia. But I honestly couldn't see why everyone was going crazy over this. This magical battle of modern times was to the ancient times as slime is to a dragon. All these matches weren't the least bit interesting—except for any fights involving my beloved daughter, Ireena, and my lone apprentice, Ginny, of course.

I knew that as their guardian and master, I should be praying for their victories, but I was hoping for the diametric opposite to prevent Operation: Instructor Ard from progressing any further.

I was praying that they lost—as quickly as possible and without injury. But the two continued to excel and tear through the ranks.

"Whew! Ireena is displaying great potential! Despite the grueling mental conditions, the other students can't get anywhere near her!"

The MCs were reviewing the most recent match during a short break, their voices amplified with a revolver-shaped sorcery device.

Weiss smiled brightly in response. "She was born with talent, but…I have to admit that Ard's teachings were a major influence."

Huh? W-wait. What is he—?

"You see, Ard acted as her mentor for a few years after they met. I always heard her talk about his lessons and principles…which were all remarkable. I was honestly a bit frightened by his ability to teach her, especially for his young age," Weiss continued, glancing at me…and winking.

Thanks for nothing! Stop looking like you're doing me a big favor by preaching about me to the world! And quit oversharing or else!

"…Oh yeah. Now that I think about it, wasn't my stupid brother a great teacher, too? *(Smile.)*"

I knew this would happen! See what you did to me, you idiot?! Back in my day, I would have had your head!

I knew that if Ginny and Ireena won, they would yap on and on about me during their postgame interview…which meant that their obnoxious operation would come to fruition.

That said, I couldn't think of a single good plan…and the final round was upon us before I knew it.

Ireena and Ginny were set to clash onstage.

In a circular field at the center of the stadium, the two glared at each other in a face-off.

"Hmph. Looks like this might be a battle to remember."

"…I agree."

Their match didn't just catch my attention but that of everyone else in the stadium. I would be relieved if they could just wrap this up without anyone getting too hurt.

As for Operation: Instructor Ard…I wasn't going to think about that anymore. I was just gonna turn a blind eye to reality.

The curtain was about to rise on the main event of the day—the last and greatest battle.

"*Aaaaaaaaaaaah?!*"

A shrill scream pierced the air, sudden and without warning, as booming sounds of destruction and angry bellows echoed from every corner, near and far.

What's going on? I thought to myself, shocked by the surprise attack.

I surveyed the area to find hordes of demons committing nothing less than atrocities in the stadium seats. The arena was in complete pandemonium, but I could see that this wasn't the only place in total chaos. When I looked far off in the distance, I spotted black smoke rising in the sky.

"Looks like we weren't their only target," noted a sonorous voice. It was Jessica.

I hadn't realized she'd been standing there scowling in the same direction as I was.

"…I'm guessing you're going to act, right, Ard? I can help out. You're coming, too, right, Lady Olivia?"

"Of course." Olivia nodded grimly and said no more.

Weiss and my parents were looking down on us, apparently having overheard our entire conversation.

"We're comin', too!"

"Hee-hee-hee, maybe I could go all out—for the first time in, like, forever!"

"Please don't. You'll blow away the capital."

Amid the screams, howls, and repulsive sounds of annihilation, the three remained blasé as ever. As expected of great heroes. They were brimming with courage.

"Carla, Weiss, and I will take care of the punks in the stadium here!" my father announced.

"Which leaves us to take care of the outside," Olivia finished.

"In that case, Olivia and Aid, handle that solo. I'm bringing Ireena and Ginny along with me for backup. I'm guessing the other students are too exhausted to help, and I'm sure the instructors will move of their own accord," Jessica suggested.

I had no objections: Jessica's plan seemed the most efficient.

But if I could have it my way...I wouldn't want Ireena to be in this fight. That said, I knew that even if I demanded that she stay, she'd jump into action whether I liked it or not.

If they were going to participate, I wanted the two of them to be close to me, especially because it seemed they were being targeted by the demons... But I assumed that Ginny wouldn't be easily swayed, much less Ireena.

On top of that, I knew we would be more efficient and save more people by splitting up. And Ireena was the kind to disregard danger to herself for the sake of helping others. This was something that I'd never be able to change in her mind.

Jessica must have noticed my somber mood, because she firmly patted my shoulder with a smile. "Relax. I may not be like you, but I'm from the household of a famous marquis, remember? I'll bring Ireena and Ginny back without a scratch on them."

"...I entrust them to your care, Jessica," I said with a single nod before issuing everyone instructions. "Are we ready to go?"

We silently got to work, and I invoked a floating spell, soaring above the stadium. With the capital spread out before me, I could see that calamity had erupted all over, just as I'd feared.

"Seriously...?! Why'd things turn out this way...?!" I clicked my tongue and headed toward a nearby area to start exterminating the enemy en masse.

Though their forces were large in number, they were pitifully weak for demons and looked virtually indistinguishable from one another. It was almost as if someone had made multiple clones of one original. Well, at any rate, it was unbelievably easy to annihilate them.

I sped through the center of the capital, indeterminately tossing attack spells at any enemy in sight for a total of thirty boring minutes—and I could see that I was starting to quell the chaos.

I guess our unit of mages was away on business or something, but whatever. If I could continue on at this rate, I knew I'd have order restored in an hour.

"This seems like a good time to check up on Ireena and the others," I mumbled, invoking *Search*, a spell to probe the surrounding area.

"Ard!" called out a familiar voice. It was my father, Jack.

When I spun around to look him in the eye, I saw that his face was colored with anxiety, which made my heart beat out of my chest.

"H-hurry! This way! Or else…," he started before signaling worse things yet to come.

"Or else *that person* will die!"

CHAPTER 18
The Ex–Demon Lord, Absent

◇◆◇

Rewind to Ireena and Ginny glowering at each other in the center of the stadium.

As the surprise attack wreaked havoc on the arena, their hostility toward each other instantly dissolved, and they were left standing there completely bewildered until Jessica made her way over to them and explained the situation. Following her proposed plan, Ireena and Ginny sprinted off to the town, raring to save the day.

Not that their turn ever came.

"*Lightning Blast*," chanted Jessica, conjuring a magic circle at her fingertips that shot out a blinding flash of lightning.

It crashed into the demon, scorching his entire body black.

"All right, let's keep it up," she remarked with a composed smile, sprinting through the streets with her platinum-blond hair dancing behind her in the wind.

The moment they encountered an enemy, Jessica would cast an attack spell without chanting and take it down in one hit before moving on to the next target. She was the spitting image of a Valkyrie, a maiden of war. As she carved a path with the ferocity of a lioness, Ireena and Ginny were completely awed by her show of force.

They continued to cover a wide range, but Ireena and Ginny didn't have an opportunity to strike as Jessica continued to settle things all on her own. The two exchanged a few words as they observed their teacher's work.

"Sh-she's amazing."

"I-I'm seeing her in a whole new light…"

Jessica let out a chuckle as she dashed through the main street, seemingly having overheard parts of their conversation. "Ha-ha, you'll be able to handle this much soon enough. If you feel up to it—"

The area around them grew dim in the middle of her sentence. They noticed shadows of a falling object inflate in size as it rained down from the sky.

"Jump out of the way!" screamed Jessica.

Ireena and Ginny had both leaped to opposite sides without her prompting, followed by their teacher, managing to escape from the scene. Their hair billowed wildly around them.

*Booooom…*echoed the heavy sounds of destructive impact, completely pulverizing the cobblestones on the streets and sending fragments scattering toward the sky. Thick smoke billowed upward as the three glared at their newest visitor, on guard.

To put it in simple terms, the enemy was a conglomeration of countless blue fragments in the shape of a human figure. His size was easily beyond three merel…

But it wasn't just his stature that'd instilled fear in their hearts. This demon was insanely tough…!

"Stay back, you two. This one's mine," ordered Jessica, letting her usual cheerful facade crumble with worry.

After Jessica confirmed with both of them with a nod, she thrust out her left hand toward the intended target.

"*Giga Flare!*" she shouted, releasing a high-level fire attack spell without a chant and calling forth eight magic circles to expand in front of her.

In the next moment, flames billowed out of each one, making a whirlpool that converged into a colossal ball of fire that closed in on the enemy, rendering the demon immobile.

It was a direct hit, engulfing the enemy's massive body in bright-red hellfire.

""Sh-she did it!"" Ireena and Ginny cheered, certain of Jessica's victory.

But that was when the flames died out, reaching the limits of their invocation, and all three faces took on a look of utter despair.

The demon was completely unharmed among his surroundings, which had been burned to a crisp in the line of fire. This caused even Jessica to break into a cold sweat.

"Damn, I'm at a loss here. This guy's beyond my—," she let out weakly, just as the body of the enemy seemed to waver and reappear right before her.

Ireena and Ginny looked absolutely aghast as expected, but Jessica couldn't help but take on an expression of absolute disbelief herself. And then his fists whizzed toward her without mercy.

She couldn't escape. He'd come at her at the exact same time as he closed the distance between them. Just before impact, Jessica cast the mid-level defense magic *Mega Wall*, but even then, the enemy's fists overpowered her.

"Gah!" she yelped as her body went flying.

The impact left some of her clothes in shreds as Jessica soared, tracing a parabola through the air before crashing down on the ground. But there was enough kinetic energy left in her body that she continued to roll and roll and roll…until it expended itself at last. Jessica didn't even move a muscle, lying completely still in her tattered clothes as if a corpse.

"*Haaah… Haaah… Haaah…*"

Ireena was dripping with sweat out of extreme fear and anxiety. Across from her, Ginny was in the same condition, and neither of them could move as the demon ambled closer to them and caught sight of Ireena.

"…My highest priority on this mission is to capture you. If you cooperate, I'll cease my attack. What say you?" he asked, continuing before she could answer. "But if you choose to flail around, all roads lead to death."

Clunk. Clunk. His heavy footsteps echoed closer.

As for Ginny, she was still stuck in place, even as Ireena was facing imminent danger right in front of her eyes. And yet, she was immobilized by fear, and her eyes pooled with tears, seemingly ashamed of her ineptitude.

On the other hand, Ireena herself was surprisingly calm.

It's hopeless.

I'm already done for.

For a moment, she felt almost composed, resigning herself to her fate, as the enemy stood directly in front of her.

"You're the cornerstone to fulfilling our dearest wish. Rejoice, young girl. For you are—," uttered the demon, delivering something akin to a death sentence.

"Don't touch my daughter," warned a voice with icy frigidity before the demon was blown away, breaking into crystalized fragments that shot through the air as if he'd received a devastating blow.

But Ireena had zero interest in the demon's condition, zeroing in on the person who'd called out to her instead.

"D-Daaaaaaaaaaaaddy!"

Standing there was an androgynous elf with silver hair that fluttered in the wind. It was the Heroic Baron, Weiss, whose piercing gaze locked onto the crumbling demon.

"Gu…wah…?!" mumbled the demon, face on the ground as if he'd been pinned down.

His entire body was crumbling to dust by the second, even though the power responsible for his destruction was unseen. Well, that'd be the case for anyone who didn't know any better. I imagine they'd guess that his body was blasted away and broke apart of its own accord.

The truth behind this phenomenon (i.e., Weiss) was a system of attack spells that generated a wind projectile, which he'd managed to develop for his exclusive use from the most recent scientific advancements.

To start, he'd manipulate the wind pressure, then crush his opponents by putting his full weight on them. It was like being stepped on by an invisible giant, which was why Weiss had named this spell *Skeleton Giant*.

"Think of this pressure as the weight of your sins for laying a hand on my daughter." His icy gaze bored into the crystallized monster. "Let your sins crush you and embrace death. That's what you deserve," he started before raising the capacity of his spell.

"A-*uuuuaaaaaaaargh!*" roared the demon, unleashing his death throes as every last crystal turned to dust and scattered in the wind.

This was more than enough to be certain of victory.

"I—I can't believe he defeated that demon so easily…! The Heroic Baron is amazing…!"

"Heh-heh-heh! Well, duh! He's my daddy, after all!" Ireena puffed her chest out proudly, dashing over to her father, about to leap into his arms.

"That was as I'd expected, more or less."

No sooner had a familiar, lovely voice rang out than a hand burst through Weiss's chest.

No, not a new appendage. Someone had attacked him from behind.

"What?" Ireena said at the sight of her father vomiting blood, collapsing to the ground with his eyes frozen open.

Her brain shut down. Over his crumpled body, his attacker came into full view.

"Whoa, whoa, whoa. Don't tell me he's on the verge of death after one measly surprise attack. Kids these days are pathetic," mumbled a girl, sounding totally bored as she licked her right hand, which was soaked in fresh blood.

It was Jessica, the instructor at the academy.

Ginny stared in shock at her sudden act of violence.

It was as if everything about their teacher had completely changed—from her behavior to her tone of voice—into a different person altogether. But that wasn't what came as the greatest surprise: It was Jessica's right hand.

The bloody hand was covered in bright-white scales with enormous nails stretching from the tips of her fingers. They were much larger than a normal human's nails, with a peculiar resemblance to the claws of predators.

"Miss Jessica...?!" Ginny whimpered.

Jessica smiled sweetly. "I ain't your 'Miss Jessica.' Well, I have been the one dealing with you guys, so technically I am your 'Jessica'... but the real lady died a long time ago. At the hands of the demons."

"What...?!" Ginny blurted, absolutely unsettled.

Jessica cackled mockingly. "I'm working with Lars al Ghoul. To help out with their plan, I entered the academy as Lady Jessica. That's right... It was all so we could abduct you, Ireena."

Ireena was tossed back into the conversation, but her brain was still completely shut down, totally incapable of processing a single thought. All she could do was tremble as she stared at the body of her fallen father.

She spoke almost unconsciously. "Why?! Why did you...?! You— you inhuman...!"

Jessica roared with laughter. "Ah-ha-ha-ha-ha! Thanks for asking a question worth answering! First question! You're wondering why I'd do something like this?! That's an easy one! I want to end the world! This repulsive planet is better off being completely annihilated! Ever since *my rampage thousands of years ago*, that's been my only guiding principle!" Her delicate and dollish features twisted with malice.

"Second, you said I was inhuman, right? You got that right. After all, I'm not actually human—I'm a white dragon."

As if to prove her point, Jessica's body began to transform, covering her left hand in scales to match her right. The unmistakable claws of a beast protruded from her fingertips, and the right corner of her adorable little mouth ripped up all the way to her ear as its round teeth tapered off into sharp points. By all accounts, she was inhuman—a complete monster.

Ginny and Ireena felt an icy chill, though it wasn't from the horror of her grotesque appearance alone: It was because Jessica was emanating an immense force from her body, draining every last ounce of energy from the pair and forcing them to submit. It immobilized the girls.

Weiss might have managed to defeat a monster...but he had the power of an ant compared to Jessica. She was on a different level altogether.

"M-monster...!" Ginny murmured.

Jessica's cracked mouth twisted into a smile. "Yep, that's right. I'm the real deal...the one from your legends. Have you heard of me? You treat me as the go-to villain in your little plays."

As she cackled, she revealed the truth.

"My true name is Elzard, the Frenzied King of Dragons."

Ireena's and Ginny's eyes practically popped out of their heads. Elzard. The Frenzied King of Dragons. The legendary white dragon... and the monster who'd nearly destroyed the world after the passing of the Demon Lord thousands of years ago. For generations, stories of this dragon had been passed down, treated with the same trepidation as the demons and the Evil Gods.

And now, this legendary creature was right here before them, and they were terrified beyond belief.

"Ah...ah...," Ginny whimpered as she fell to her knees.

Jessica—no, Elzard cast a sidelong glance at her before approaching Ireena and fanning her arms out wide.

"It sucks to repeat the lines of a bottom-tier monster, but here it goes... If you come willingly, I promise not to hurt anyone, okay? Well, for the time being, at least," she corrected, the corners of her gaping maw twitching as she edged closer and closer.

It's over for me for real this time. Ireena resigned herself to her fate.

"Argh... *Aaaaaaaaaaaaaah!*" erupted a scream, at the same time as a fireball came crashing into the side of Elzard's face, detonating upon impact.

But any damage to the dragon was nonexistent, though she cocked her eyebrow at this surprise development.

"...What exactly do you plan on doing, Ginny?" she asked, glaring down at the succubus for unleashing her magic.

One look was enough to make Ginny falter and send her onto one knee, but she continued to launch more fireballs at her target even as she heaved out labored breaths. Her eyes were dewy with absolute horror.

"R-run, Miss Ireena!" she demanded in a trembling voice between attacks.

All of them collided into her target, but she was in such a tortured mental state that her spells were no threat to Elzard.

"Well, well, well. The one too scared to go against that dinky demon is coming after me. Why? Do I look that pathetic? ...I really don't like you," Elzard spat as she continued to be pummeled by fireballs, glaring at Ginny like she was a particularly annoying fly.

When Elzard lifted the tip of the claw on her right index finger at

Ginny, images of the succubus's impending death flashed through Ireena's mind. Her brain was no longer blank but colored by red-hot rage.

"*Aaaaaaaaaaaargh!*"

Ireena had let out a scream unconsciously, charging at her former instructor and trying to tackle her down at her waist. But it wasn't enough to even budge Elzard's body.

"...What do you think you're doing?"

In all honesty, Ireena herself had no idea why she was protecting Ginny. It wasn't as if she could say that it was in alignment with her personality, because Ireena found Ginny deplorable for coming in between her and Ard. And yet, at this moment, Ireena felt compelled to save Ginny from the very bottom of her heart.

Why? Ireena asked herself, completely at a loss, but there was something in her heart that answered back on impulse.

"*Don't you dare! Touch my friend!*" she shouted, going bug-eyed at the words that came instinctively rushing out of her mouth.

Friend? Did I just say that Ginny and I are friends?

...Yeah, I guess we might be.

After all, Ginny had taken a special place in Ireena's life, out of everyone she'd met so far. When they were together, Ireena never needed to hold back any spitefulness or fears or worries, since Ginny was the most detestable woman in her mind—nothing more, nothing less.

This might be another form of friendship, Ireena considered and broke out into a small smile.

"Take me with you, Elzard! But in return, promise you won't lay a finger on Ginny! If you do, I'll bite my tongue off and kill myself!" Ireena declared, pelting Elzard with newfound determination.

Elzard could sense that it was no bluff, heaving out a huge sigh.

"...Damn, what a pain. I really do hate you after all," she mumbled to herself.

With that, Elzard busted through the remainder of the tattered clothes that had been clinging to her back as a pair of wings ruptured out of the surface of her smooth, exposed skin.

"Looks like your life's been spared. Isn't that great, Ginny?" she said sarcastically as her final words before taking off into the sky with Ireena clutched in one hand.

Ginny stood alone and dazed for some time.

"Miss Ireena...!" she finally sobbed out.

A cascade of emotions welled up inside her before she noticed she was weeping uncontrollably.

CHAPTER 19
The Ex–Demon Lord and a Plan to Attack

Or else that person will die.

Jack had been the one to deliver these disquieting words to me, and I followed him with mounting anxiety to our destination, the nurse's office at the academy. It was almost serene in there, unlike the chaos currently wreaking havoc on the city.

Count Golde was next to the bed, casting healing spells on… Weiss and looking absolutely fraught with despair. But as soon as he caught sight of me, it dissolved into a look of hope.

"Oh! Thank goodness you're here, Ard! You'll be able to heal Weiss, right?!"

Both Golde and Jack simultaneously gave off a "chop, chop! get to it!" vibe, so I nodded once and approached Weiss, who was half-naked with no external wounds. I assumed Golde had sealed those up with his spells, but Weiss's face was pallid, and he seemed to be on the verge of death.

But that was no biggie. I faced my right palm toward his body, casting *Heal*, a low-level spell, and witnessed the color returning to his face in no time—until he finally opened his eyes.

"Where am I…?!" Weiss asked, sitting up in his bed and scanning the room with a wild expression.

But it didn't take him too long to assess the situation. He shot a quick glance at Jack and Golde, who were both giddy with glee.

"I would thank you if I had time," he apologized before turning to me. "I'll be brief. My daughter, Ireena…has been abducted."

"…Ah, I thought as much."

It may have been what I'd expected, but this news stabbed me in my heart.

Weiss continued on without any regard for my shift in mood. "It's…Elzard, the Frenzied King of Dragons, who took Ireena. It seems she infiltrated the academy disguised as Jessica, all the while joining forces with the demons and scheming to destroy the world…"

…I see. So Jessica was the traitor, I thought to myself, but I wasn't all that surprised in truth. I'd noticed something fishy about her for some inexplicable reason. But I hadn't had solid proof, which meant I hadn't been able to take drastic measures to kick her out of the academy.

But…to think that her true form was Elzard.

"Whoa, gimme a break. First an Evil God, then the Frenzied King of Dragons? One mythical enemy is plenty…," Jack noted. The sweat on his face was telling.

"I-isn't there some sort of mistake? Could it be a phony passing themselves off as Elzard?" Golde suggested, looking dubious.

Weiss let out a labored sigh and shook his head. "My consciousness was drifting in and out, but I managed to assess her fighting abilities. I'd say she's comparable to the Evil God we destroyed a decade ago… No, maybe even more powerful."

Golde fell into silence, along with Jack. All three looked forlorn. When it came down to it, this was a difficult situation. That said, what we had to do was simple.

"All we have to do is think about how to bring Ireena back. The strength of our enemies doesn't change our goal," I muttered before asking Weiss the one question that'd been bothering me for a while.

"By the way, why in the world did the demons abduct Ireena? I noticed they've been targeting her for some time. I assumed it was to get revenge against the heroes who defeated the Evil God, but this incident takes that too far. Could there be an ulterior motive?"

Weiss was quiet for a moment.

"We carry the Olhyde name...but it's an alias. All of this talk about Baron Olhyde, the one who rules the remote border villages, is a front. My real name is..." He paused for a second before continuing with a decisive look. "Laville. In other words, this nation's true royal family."

"Hmm. Got it."

"...A-aren't you surprised?"

"I'm just not showing it."

If I were your average human, I guess now would be the time to express shock. But you have to remember that I'm the ex–Demon Lord who's lived close to a thousand years in another life. This wasn't enough to throw me off my A game.

"That said, Weiss, even if you're the actual king and Ireena is the princess...it still doesn't explain why the demons would take things this far. Let's say they abducted Ireena to use her as a bargaining piece for some cause. I still can't figure out what they're after. Which makes me believe you're hiding something else. Am I wrong?"

Weiss gave a pained look and said nothing.

Golde patted his shoulders. "I think we can tell Ard now. Don't you? There's no one more trustworthy than him," he persuaded.

Weiss nodded with newfound resolve. "We...the Laville family... carry the blood of the Evil Gods...!"

His expression said he'd planned on taking this to his grave.

On the other side, Golde and Jack seemed to know this truth, as they kept their composure and looked pointedly at me.

So what? That was my honest-to-goodness reaction to all this.

"A-aren't you shocked by this news?"

"I'm surprised, but...everything makes sense now. And that outweighs my shock. Ireena was targeted because she carries the blood of the Evil Gods. It's all coming together. I'm guessing the demons are planning on using her as a sacrifice in their ceremony to resurrect the Evil Gods. She's a perfect fit, since she carried their bloodline, and they targeted her over you, because she hasn't matured as a mage yet. Yeah. All the pieces finally fit," I concluded.

The three stared openmouthed at my torrential monologue.

"Bwa-ha-ha-ha-ha! That's my son all right! Ya see, Weiss? He's sayin' there's nothin' to worry about!" Jack thumped Weiss's back with a hearty laugh.

"I never imagined someone other than us would take this news in stride... Well, I reckon blood will tell." Golde fiddled with his goatee with a wry smile.

"...I'm relieved," Weiss murmured, looking like a heavy burden had been lifted off his shoulders.

Well, I guess this would be a huge revelation for any normal person. But to me, it was like, *And? What about it?*

In my old life, I'd met a number of people who carried the blood of the Evil Gods, including my own subordinates...and my best friend in that lifetime, Lydia the Champion, which explained my total lack of reaction.

Weiss dropped more tidbits. "Because we worship the Demon Lord as our chief deity, any connection to the Evil Gods immediately becomes a target for utter disgust and loathing. If it came out that the royal family carried their blood in its lineage...the government would be overthrown without a doubt. This blood is a blessing and a curse. It makes our family gifted. That's why the nation is better off in our hands."

This was a predicament of all predicaments: It was clear that a nation should be run by the most superior, qualified individuals, but they were the ones who'd be the most discriminated against in this generation.

"That's why our ancestors created this system. The 'royal family' facing the general public is made up of puppets, running everything on the surface while the true royal family gives their input on all the big decisions in the shadows... I think a new system is long overdue, but I haven't been able to come up with the right solution."

I began to see that some hardships could be understood only by true kings like Weiss, who'd cast his eyes downward and sighed despondently.

I replied with a simple "I see" before returning to the topic at hand.

"Well, Weiss, I'd like you to grant me access to the treasure vault in the palace. I know this is rude of me, but I have to make it clear that this is an order, not a request. I'm sorry to ask this when you've just recovered, but you've got to move," I said curtly.

Weiss seemed to feel the same way, replying, "I leave it to you," as he quietly got up from the bed.

As we went to leave the room, Golde called out from behind us. "Wh-what are you planning on doing, Ard?!"

"What do I plan to do? Pick up my friend, and that's it."

"H-how can you be so calm...?" Golde looked at me blankly for a moment before screwing up his face. "I don't wanna say this, but we're talkin' about Elzard, y'know? Even you..."

Er, sure. More like, Elzard who?

To Golde and other people from modern times, Elzard was a famous white dragon—a single entity with an immense presence. But to me, she was nothing more than a ginormous lizard. Like any other dragon. Then again, I was much weaker now than in my heyday. It'd be a tough fight for sure.

That said, I wasn't so weak that some wannabe lizard could fling me around as her plaything. Not that I'd say that out loud. I knew trouble followed when I made those kinds of statements. It was what it was.

I thrust out my chest. "Count Golde. Please allow me to inform you," I declared, loud and proud, "(Demon) Lord knows, the word *impossible* isn't in my lexicon."

...Thanks to Weiss pulling some strings, I was able to enter the treasure vault underground with Weiss and Queen Rosa, who was actually a stand-in for the real royal family. The inner vault was lined with shelves that held a magnificent bunch of national treasures.

A few of them stood out to me: an overcoat, the color of the void. A crimson spear. A pair of azure greaves. These were exactly what I was looking for.

They were known as the Armor of the Demon Lord, or powerful magical equipment made up of 666 pieces that I'd personally crafted in my past life.

In my will, I'd instructed that these pieces be spread out to every corner of the globe. I'd left them as a trump card, should any Evil Gods resurrect after my death. It seemed my subordinates had followed these instructions perfectly. This country was currently safeguarding three of them as national treasures.

"Ard Meteor. What exactly are thee planning to do with those? Am I safe to assume thee cannot wield the Armor of the Demon Lord?"

"Yes, most certainly not. That would be impossible," I admitted.

It wasn't a matter of me refusing to be the center of attention. I mean, even in old-world standards, these weapons were configured to be unusable to anyone other than extremely high-level mages. With my body now, my magical power would completely dry up if I handled one piece of weaponry, let alone three.

"I can't use them as is, which is why I'll transform them into armor more appropriate for my current abilities."

""...Huh?""

Rosa looked at me with wide eyes—and even Weiss was shocked.

"Did I say something surprising? These may be called the Armor of the Demon Lord, but they're no different from any other magical equipment, right? They're weaponry that's been imbued with special characteristics using an attribution spell, more or less. That also means it's possible to rewrite them to create something usable."

"Nay, nay, nay! In theory, perhaps, but no one has ever been able to accomplish that! Thy must know that rewriting a magical formula requires a perfect understanding of the inner workings of these attributes!"

"Plus, it wasn't a random mage who worked on these weapons but the Demon Lord himself, which means their spells must be complex and bizarre... I've heard that many have gone mad attempting to understand them," Weiss vocalized with skepticism.

Rosa was looking like she was totally convinced that I'd never be able to manage this feat as I proceeded to rewrite the techniques before their very eyes.

"*Open. Door of Essence.*" I recited two incantations, causing geometric patterns to fly out of the three pieces, creating six-merel magic circles before one another.

If you considered the fact that magic circles in this era were less than ten celti on average, the size of these went above and beyond the norm. I glanced over the four magical formulas contained within these magic circles, pointing my finger toward them—to begin rewriting them super smoothly.

""Wait, hold on, what?"" Rosa and Weiss were once again in harmony.

I heard snippets of their conversation as they yapped on behind me: "I was told it'd be impossible for anyone but the Demon Lord to decipher these techniques" and "I shall make thee my husband after all."

I ignored all their comments, writing with utter indifference to lower the capacities of the weapons into a more appropriate level for my current self. As for the greaves, I changed their composition entirely. They were originally made to allow the user to move at high speed, but now I was rewriting the formula so they would let me fly ultrafast instead before continuing on with more mods.

"You really do defy all common sense," Weiss noted with a wry smile. "That must be why she's so taken by you," he added before letting out a little sigh. "It might be hard to believe because she's so different now, but until she met you, she used to lock herself away in the mansion."

My work halted for a moment when I realized what he was saying.

"Back then, any stranger was a source of fear, because she knew out of instinct that no one could ever find out about our secret. She was certain they'd all persecute her one day… She's changed thanks to you. But it was so terrible when she was little."

Ireena's secret wasn't a big deal from my perspective. But it had been enough for her to regret being born and possessing this special quality. And I mean that in a bad way.

Ireena never let on that she was bearing this heavy burden, flashing her eternally bright smile whenever she was in my company.

...I wonder how much pain was lying just behind that smile, I thought, feeling as though my heart would burst open from my chest.

"After the two of you met, Ireena started venturing outside every day. And she even made the decision to attend the academy... To tell you the truth, I'd lived through similar days in my past. That's why I fretted, worrying myself sick about whether she'd be able to live a full life. But now, I'm not concerned in the least. I know I already said this before, but...it's all thanks to you, Ard," he offered, just as I finished modifying these weapons.

Weiss could guess what was to come and gave me a hardened look. "If the demons succeed, there'll be major casualties, and even more than that...Ireena will die. I refuse to accept that. She has so much going for her. I mean, her life's just begun," he continued with his fists balled up tightly.

He bowed his head. "I know I'm the so-called Heroic Baron or whatever, but I can't even save my own daughter... Save her in place of her pathetic father. Please."

Queen Rosa piped up before I could reply. "She's an enigma. She swam straight into my heart. When I first met her, I was vexed by her timidity...but now she's my one and only true friend. I request this of thee, too. Save Ireena," she finished, bowing her head next to Weiss.

I smiled at the two and gave my answer. "Leave it to me. After all, I wish to save...my friend, who's more precious than life itself."

I wanted to see that smile again. I would save her no matter what.

...Even if our relationship ended as a result.

I equipped myself with the Armor of the Demon Lord before leaving the treasure vault and exiting the palace grounds.

"Ard!" I heard someone shout and saw Ginny approach me with her peach-colored hair swishing behind her.

I assumed she'd been trying to find me and dashing all around, as she came toward me with heaving, ragged breaths and sweat streaming out of her body like small waterfalls.

"You're gonna…save Miss Ireena…right?"

"Yes, but things are going to get dangerous this time around… and I won't let you accompany me," I ordered.

Ginny hung her head as she assumed a cloudy expression, staying silent for a few moments until she finally managed to slowly string together her words.

"You helped me find my strength, Ard… You gave me confidence…and I thought I'd changed. But…I still couldn't make any friends. I honestly gave up all hope and assumed I'd never be able to improve this one thing… I thought I was gonna die alone with no friends and continue to be lonely forever. But…" Ginny stopped for a moment as tears started to form in her eyes.

"But Miss Ireena…called me her friend…!" Big globs of tears cascaded down her beautiful face, which had become crumpled with sadness.

"She called…someone like me…her friend…! That's why…!" she shouted, sobbing now. *"You have to save Miss Ireena!"*

She ducked her head with force, bowing in front of me. I swept my eyes from her to a clock tower in the distance and gave her the tiniest of smiles.

"Hmm. We may make dinnertime. Well then, Ginny. How about you cook some curry while you're waiting for our return? I'm guessing Ireena is going to be famished."

As I allowed magic to flow into the greaves of my armor, I invoked a spell, rising gently into the air. I prepared to soar into the sky when I suddenly remembered one last thing.

"Ah, right. You just said you didn't have any friends. Don't you realize that, along with Ireena, I consider you a friend, too?"

Ginny looked up at me with eyes as round as saucers.

My smile stretched a bit farther as I called out to her. "When Ireena comes back, let's be silly and laugh again."

"…Yeah!" she exclaimed with tears in her eyes, but I could tell these weren't from sorrow. I flashed a grin upon seeing Ginny beam through her tears.

And then I raced toward the night sky stained in darkness, shooting upward with all my might.

CHAPTER 20
The Ex–Demon Lord Versus the Frenzied King of Dragons, Elzard

◇◆◇

The Vylamd Mountain Range was a large belt of peaks that stretched along the northernmost tip of the Laville Empire of Sorcery. It was known as the domain of Elzard, the Frenzied King of Dragons, and humans dared not step foot in it. Even monsters didn't approach its vicinity.

Since ancient times, these mountains had been the home of the white dragons. It'd once been called a paradise of dragons because they would choose to rest their wings here... That was until Elzard massacred all of her brethren, leaving her its sole resident.

There was one extraordinarily tall mountain within the home region of this blood-soaked creature, boasting a towering summit even when compared to the rest. Its crown pierced through clouds and extended into the reaches of space itself.

This peak was known as the sleeping quarters of the King of Dragons. There, the demons were proceeding with a ceremony to summon the Evil God. The faint glow of the moon and stars emerged out of the pitch darkness of space, casting an eerie luminosity on the scene.

On the extensive and flat terrain, an enormous special-class magic circle had been transposed onto the earth. And at the center

of it all was Ireena, chained to an altar and soaking in sweat. She'd
been completely stripped of all clothing, lying there exposed without
a stitch on her as she sweated profusely, beads forming on her supple, pale skin. Her mountainous breasts rose and fell in time with her
breathing.

There was an enormous monster lying in wait beside her, squirming anxiously—or in anticipation of the maiden's body. It was known
as the Orphan of Chaos. Simply put, it was a tentacle monster.

There were countless arms that thrashed and wiggled around,
stretching out of a sphere in the center of the mass that housed a giant
eyeball. It leered at Ireena, who was tense with fear.

The Orphan of Chaos had been stitched together from the corpo-
real remnants of the Evil Gods before they'd all been obliterated by
the Demon Lord Varvatos.

By joining the blood and physical body of the Evil Gods together in
a sacrifice, the demons could summon one of the calamities sealed in an
alternate dimension. In other words, they could complete this ceremony
by using Ireena, who had inherited a portion of the soul of an Evil God,
and the Orphan of Chaos. Their preparations were complete.

The demons were letting their energy flow into the huge magic
circle underfoot, while Elzard looked upon its dim purple glow. Then
she glanced over at their faces, which were marked with anxiety. The
mood was heavy. That was to be expected. After all, their dreams were
about to come true before their very eyes.

And at long last, the magic circle finished charging up.

Elzard smirked and approached Ireena strapped to the altar. "Hey
there, Ireena. How ya doin'?"

Ireena's tearful eyes narrowed as she glared at her captor.

Serves you right, Elzard thought. *This is for growing up in a loving
environment, even though you're a monster—just like me.*

But now, Ireena had been cast into the pits of hell, which gave
great pleasure to Elzard, who was spurred on by her sadistic heart.

"Turn your head up... There. Can you see? Yeah, that disgusting tentacle monster. It's going to rape you."

"Rape me...?" Ireena parroted, unsure of what that meant, as her eyes swam around in discomposure.

"Let me walk you through it. These tentacles are going to enter each and every orifice of your body—mouth, nose, and ears, of course...plus your ass—and here," continued Elzard as she traced Ireena's lower half with a finger.

When it trailed down to her private parts, Ireena went ghost white...but she managed to muster up her courage.

"I'm not scared! At all! 'Cause I know Ard's gonna come and save me!" she shouted with an expression that displayed absolute faith in a certain boy.

Ireena seemed so certain that her friend would never betray her, absolutely sure of her convictions, which reminded Elzard of her own past...

How intolerable. **I want to destroy her.** The corners of Elzard's mouth strung upward as she delivered lines certain of satisfying these desires.

"Sure, you'd be safe if Ard swooped in. For a moment. But is that what you want? Because I'd have to tell him every last one of your secrets, y'know."

Ireena's eyes snapped open wide and stared at Elzard without a single trace of bravery on her face. It was as if she wanted to beg *Please! Anything but that*, which made Elzard grin all the more.

"Ard might have superhuman strength...but he's a human all the same. I mean, he's a product of this era. Which means... Well, I don't need to spell it out. He's just the same as everyone else. If he finds out your secret, he'll hate you—despise you as a monster."

Ireena had no reply to this. There were things she wanted to say: *He's not that kind of person* or *he's my lifelong friend* or *he'd never betray me*.

Just like me, thought Elzard.

But Ireena couldn't get herself to utter any of these things—even Ard wasn't exempt from these doubts. She couldn't place her absolute confidence in him.

It made sense. To reveal her secret was akin to dropping a bomb. That's how serious it was, which Elzard knew all too well. She chuckled darkly—evilly.

"If he doesn't come and save you, you're gonna die after you're completely violated. If he does, you're gonna lose your one and only friend. Meaning...your life is over either way," Elzard whispered in Ireena's ear as her dollish features twisted wickedly. "My condolences. ♪"

This might have been the point when Ireena finally realized this was checkmate. Her mask of bravado peeled away and...revealed the face of a pitiful victim—ghastly pale and shaking in fear of the fate that awaited her.

There was a part of Elzard that had her desire perfectly satisfied by this situation, but she was craving more.

"Move the Orphan of Chaos. Let's start this ceremony."

The demons turned their palms toward the monster to fill it with magical energy as they expressed their intentions. With that, the Orphan of Chaos wiggled its tentacles in delight and slowly made its way toward Ireena.

"No... Stop... Stay away... *Stay awaaaaaaaaaaaay!*" she shrieked, even as she lost all hope.

Ireena desperately tried to escape her bindings at the eleventh hour, bawling and screaming, but her chains were unyielding. The repulsive monster drew closer.

"*Help! Someone! Help meeeeeee!*" she wailed, excreting bodily fluids out of her privates.

Elzard continued to watch the scene with a wicked smile until the Orphan of Chaos finally reached Ireena. It squirmed its tentacles.

The slimy black appendages extended toward her feet, coiling around her legs, snaking along her supple, milky thighs, and tightening their grasp. They inched farther and farther upward.

"Ah-ha-ha-ha-ha-ha-ha! Two monsters! A match made in heaven!" Elzard cackled, her raucous laughter echoing all around.

The demons watched the ceremony with bated breath.

"*No! No, no, no! Stop it! Stop!*" Ireena cried out, trying to resist with everything she had, but her efforts were futile, no matter how much she fought and wailed.

The Orphan of Chaos's tentacles slithered onward, and its girthy, slimy thing was ready to penetrate the deepest parts of Ireena.

Just then, the monster's colossal body erupted into flames.

"*Djfadjfjfa?!*" the monster shrieked incomprehensively as most of its tentacles were blown off, sputtering green blood everywhere.

The demons and Elzard watched in momentary shock...right as something flew in at sonic speed from their periphery, impaling the monster's eye.

They collectively whipped around to locate the source.

Up in the sky, floating out in the dark vastness of space, was a single boy, cloaked in a jet-black overcoat and holding a spear in one hand. This sight threw the demons into an uproar, but Elzard scowled at him amid the tumult and barked a laugh.

"You're here...! Ard Meteor...!"

He dropped to the ground with an air of composure. As he touched down, Elzard couldn't help but think of one of the great paintings of history, *The Descent of the Demon Lord.*

"Good day, insects, one and all," he said with a chuckle as immense demonic energy seeped out of his entire body.

His aura was threatening enough to make even the legendary monster Elzard grow hot under the collar. As for the demons, they wouldn't dare lift a finger, even though they were facing but a single enemy and those present were the most elite veterans as well as survivors of the ancient world. But even they had difficulty staring back at the newcomer.

"You've really done it now," he remarked slowly, as if reprimanding a naughty child, and his crimson eyes shone brightly. "I don't intend to let a single one of you crawl away, so you'd best prepare yourselves."

With this declaration of war, Ard let his demonic aura rise to new heights, emanating unconditional strength. From the perspective of Ireena, his presence was akin to salvation itself. As for her attackers, there was nothing more terrifying, and these hardened veterans couldn't even move enough to tremble as they shed buckets of sweat.

Except for the elderly demon, their leader, who finally showed some dauntlessness. "Don't lose heart! This may be an unforeseen development, but stick to the plan and move!"

His rage stirred the others, who began to set to work with looks of fearlessness, gathering into formation in the blink of an eye.

""""*Transcendental Beings! May Thou Be Our Fierce Thunder! And Bring Down Ruin!*"""" they recited in a collective invocation.

This was a magical technique made possible from long years of group training, and its power was comparable to the collective effort required to acquire this skill.

Following these three short chants, an enormous magic circle manifested beneath the demons and...a massive pillar of light shot up from the ground.

Using the magical powers of a few dozen people, this was a special-class attack spell utilizing a language characteristic to the demons—not by using runes.

That's some powerful stuff. It would have held up even in the ancient world, noted Elzard, admiring the skills of the demons. It was amazing that they'd managed to build their strength up to this. Under the force of such magic, even the strongest would vanish without a trace.

"D-did we do it…?!"

"We put our whole bodies and souls into that shot. There's no way he could survive…!"

The demons were certain of their victory. Even Elzard felt a sense of finality.

But the pillar of light instantly disappeared as soon as the invocation had reached its limit.

"I'm terribly sorry, but playtime is over."

They all froze in place.

"H-how is he unharmed…?! Impossible…!" whispered a young demon with wide eyes.

Ard Meteor stood there in all his elegance—without a single scratch in sight. Their countless hours of study hadn't even been able to wipe the grin off his face.

"Well then… I suppose it's my turn."

He flashed a cold smile, and nine magic circles manifested around him, but he hadn't invoked multiple spells at once.

"I-is this a *Nine Cast*?!" The elderly demon was struck with wonder as the circles unleashed their magic one after the other.

Combustion. Lightning. Ice Sword. Clod. Impact. Flash. Miasma. Steel Stake. Dark Rush.

Every single attack was a violent and atrocious force to be reckoned with.

Though the demons had honed their skills through a hundred wars and each was a fearsome monster in their own right, they were all being laid to waste.

"Kill him! *Kill hiiiiiiim!*"

"*Aaaaaaah?!*"

"M-my leg! *My leeeeeg!*"

Amid the howls and screams, Ard went on exercising his power with ease, even though he was alone and surrounded by enemies in a situation that anyone else would find demoralizing. But he was as carefree as he would be strolling through a garden. A smile played on his lips as he one-sidedly defeated each and every one of the demons—all without killing them.

"Amazing...! Ard, you're incredible...!" whispered Ireena, who was bound up beside Elzard.

Her expression was a mixture of pure hope and admiration, no longer holding any fear of the demons, just like her friend.

"...Well played, Ard." Elzard began to sweat, crushed under the weight of reality.

Ard Meteor hadn't even unleashed a fraction of his real power. He was going easy on them to prevent his dearest friend from being petrified. After all, he could easily take on a horde of monsters with the strength of ten thousand soldiers.

He deviated enough from the norm for the title of Irregular to suit him.

"...Are friends that important to you? Do you not want to lose them, Ard Meteor?" Elzard murmured as she came to a single realization.

He's just how I used to be.

She'd been pathetically lonely, seeking to make friends, only to be left with a heaping pile of futile efforts. It was exactly why she understood him so well.

If he knew everything about me, I bet he'd be just as understanding. We'd be able to support each other as like-minded individuals.

This kind of presence is what I've always wished for—the relationship I've always wanted. But that's also why...

That was why...her hatred for him grew even stronger.

"Why couldn't you be born sooner?"

Everything was fatally too late. Even if her wish came true, it wouldn't do anything to ease Elzard's heart.

"If only you'd been born sooner. If only we met earlier in life...!"

she screeched, glaring at the boy as he knocked down the demons with blinding force. "Ah… It's been so long since I had this feeling…"

The bloodthirsty dragon, the one who'd been driven into a berserk fury from loneliness, clenched her hands into fists.

"You're driving me mad, Ard Meteor…!"

◇◆◇

Upon leaving the capital, I followed a trail of magical residue to find Elzard, formerly known as Jessica. She'd taken measures to cover her tracks to make sure she couldn't be tailed, and it was all starting to make sense how she'd survived from the ancient world…but she couldn't fool these eyes.

I followed them all the way to her location and promptly dealt with the disgusting clump of tentacles. It was payback time for trying to deflower my Ireena. And then I continued with wiping out the demons—well, in a manner of speaking.

"Gwah…!"

"My eyes… My eyes…!"

I didn't kill a single one. It wasn't worth taking a worthless life. That would go against my style…

Plus, it would scare Ireena if she saw me totally massacre everyone. That meant I left a handful of demons with enough strength to move around, but they didn't need to be dealt with right now. After all, I'd rendered them physically and mentally powerless.

"Well, then…," I said as I went to check on Ireena.

She was chained to a pedestal at the top of a mountain and naked from every angle.

Absolutely shameless. How dare they disgrace her in this way…! I thought to myself, brimming with pure, unbridled rage.

I stepped up to Ireena and cast a spell with a snap of my fingers, calling forth magic circles around the chains, which froze in an instant and crumbled apart with a *crack* seconds later.

"*Aaaaaaaah! Aaaaaaard!*" she screamed.

She must have been completely petrified, seeing as her usual bravado was nowhere to be found. Ireena sprinted over to me, letting her melon-size breasts swish back and forth as tears gushed out of her eyes like waterfalls.

"*I was so scaaaaaaaaared!*" she yelled, leaping into my arms.

The ends of her long silver strands of hair wagged left and right, looking like the tail of a happy puppy reuniting with its master.

...Yes, Ireena was my friend, beloved daughter, and like my little puppy.

There were two soft mounds being pressed against my chest, and her plump booty was in full view. Any normal person would have been overcome by desire, but I felt nothing of the sort. Yep. Absolutely nothing at all.

I gently held her trembling body and softly stroked her head. "It seems I was a bit late. To allow a lady to be exposed this way... I still have a long way to go," I noted with a heavy sigh.

I covered Ireena with my black overcoat, though I knew it would suck her magical powers out of her for as long as she was cloaked in it. In exchange, it would nullify attacks at a base level, and she really needed that right now.

Ireena shook her head frantically. "Th-that's not true! A-and I wasn't embarrassed at all when they saw me naked! If I'm telling you the truth...my crotch was, like, throbbing? And it kind of felt good, almost—"

"...Let us discuss the matter at length when we're home. For now—," I started to say, but I was cut off by a torrent of sharp magical energy that came flying toward us.

I reflexively tried to deflect it with my right hand, which had been fortified with defense spells, and it sent a jolt through my palm that traveled down the rest of my body.

An elementary-level spell, Lightning Shot, *huh,* I thought to myself.

It wasn't an attack meant to stop me. It was just to get my attention.

I spun around and made eye contact with my foe, Elzard. Something must have happened to her without my noticing, since her long platinum hair was slightly dingy, and her clothes were torn to shreds.

"Oh dear. How embarrassing. I bet I look a little worse for wear. I don't even have any makeup on. All my fake eyelashes and stuff flew off when I soared through the sky, you know."

"Worry about your public image, first. I can't believe you'd kidnap a sweet young maiden. Your mother in the heavens will weep if she catches wind of this."

"I dunno about that. My mother was a huge bitch."

The conversation itself was easygoing enough, but we were both wound tight.

I readied myself to go full throttle on her, and she transformed again with an aura thick with bloodlust as the skin on her hands erupted with scales. Talons extended out of her fingers, and the corners of her dainty mouth ripped all the way up to her ears, framed by two horns that sprouted from either side of her head. Elzard was emanating an extraordinarily suffocating vibe, making the air around us undulate and the earth quiver.

Her power was…equal in every way to the great ancient warriors.

"Oh…! What presence…!"

"We've been defeated, but she still stands…!"

"He may be the son of the Great Mages, but he can't possibly win against a monster of legend…!"

The light had returned to the demons' eyes, full and round with hope. On the other hand, gloom once again settled on Ireena's face.

"A-Ard…" She gripped me tighter.

I stroked her hair before I slipped my arm around her waist.

"Don't worry," I whispered. "A lizard is no challenge for me. It won't take me long to clean this up. In the meantime, think about dinner, Ireena. We've prepared your favorite curry dish tonight. I hope you're looking forward to it."

I grinned at her, which made Ireena's fear dissolve somewhat.

"Okay!" she replied and attempted to give me a weak smile, which was seriously supercute.

"Hey, hey, stop with the PDA. You really like her? Even though she's a monster?" Elzard asked, giving Ireena a once-over with a wicked smile.

…At the mention of the word *monster,* Ireena's smile disappeared completely as uneasiness came rushing back in full force.

"Y'know, that girl ain't as pretty as you think. She's actually—"

"Stop it! No more!" Ireena screamed as her blue eyes welled up with tears.

But that only seemed to rile up Elzard's sadistic nature. A devious smile stretched from ear to ear, and she looked expectant, almost, in a twisted way.

"She carries the blood of the Evil Gods. It's the truth. No mistaking it. That's why Lars al Ghoul targeted her."

Ireena's gaze pierced into me—in panic, fear, anxiety, and… despair, absolutely convinced that this revelation would obliterate our relationship. And Elzard seemed to think she'd be able to see a tragic end unfold in front of her.

I was ready to give a bold proclamation.

"That's perfectly fine."

"…What did you say?" Elzard's eyes widened, appearing surprised by my response.

Ireena's eyes just about popped out of her head, too, and I could see her expression change dramatically. To put the last bit of Elzard's scheme to rest and my friend at ease, I didn't stop there.

"If I were a normal human, my reaction would have played out as you'd expected. But I'm lacking in common sense, unfortunately. I wouldn't care if she was an Evil God or carried their blood. What matters—"

I stopped and cast my eyes on her face. I smiled down at Ireena, whose expression was marked with concern and trepidation, as I lightly stroked her trembling head.

"What matters is that she's someone worthy of my respect and affection. That's all. Ireena is more courageous and generous than anyone. I find her blinding, brilliant... Someone as bright as the sun itself. That's why I admire her—and why I can't forgive you for referring to her as a *monster*."

I looked from Ireena to Elzard with a cold ruthlessness and red-hot fury.

"Don't you dare insult my *friend*," I spat, speaking straight from the heart, as Ireena's sobs rang out.

But I didn't glance down at her. She probably wouldn't have wanted that.

From her trembling body, I could sense that she was no longer in a state of fear or panic—but rather one of joyous relief. And that alone was enough for me.

"...Hmph. Well, this was all in the realm of possibility. Whatever. I've still got lots planned ahead."

"I see. In that case, allow me to crush each one head-on." I released the arm holding Ireena. "Please stand back. Things are going to get unsafe, even with the overcoat on."

"R-right! Go show her who's boss!"

"Yes, my lady," I said, offering her a smile, and Ireena retreated farther back.

"Well. You've kidnapped my friend, stripped her, and put her through extraordinary disgrace, then sent her into the utmost limits of fear and, to top it all off, verbally assaulted her... If I take into account that your power is comparable to the ancient heroes...," I trailed off.

It was like my heart had frosted over, taking control of my lips and spilling these lines out of their own accord. It'd been ages since I felt so intoxicated. I would fight with the full force of my strength and...

"It seems you're worth killing."

Take her shameless heart. When I let myself think that, I became keenly aware of a wave of acute pleasure washing across my entire body in an unconscious release of my dark thirst for battle. It must have put Elzard on edge.

Her face gleamed with sweat. "...Geez, you're a pain in the ass to the very end," she mumbled as she readied herself. "I can't wait to see your look of total despair!" shouted Elzard, thrusting out her left hand toward me to manifest golden magic circles.

Eight of them in total. She'd activated this spell using the language of dragons, which was said to be the first vernacular used for spells.

The circles raged menacingly, launching pure-white light from each of them in the next moment and kicking up a thick cloud of dust with each direct hit. Elzard released attacks one after the other without mercy.

"Wh-what a fierce attack...!"

"As expected of the legendary white dragon...! She's on a completely different level...!"

The voices of the demons trembled with fear.

"A-Ard?!" Ireena's cry sliced through the air, presumably worried for my safety, which brought a smile to my lips.

"There's no cause for alarm. As I mentioned before...a lizard of this level is no match for me," I replied calmly.

It must have struck Elzard as a warning, because her attacks halted. The dust cleared, and I was visible for all to see.

"Wha...?!"

"H-her attack did nothing...?!"

The demons weren't the only ones who were completely confused. Elzard frowned. "...Weird. I didn't see you cast any defense spells."

"I have nothing to hide. Allow me to enlighten you: It's all thanks to this spear—which has been imbued with the power to nullify any lightning attacks."

"Huh. So that's why my magic did nothing."

We both exchanged smiles and pleasantries.

"Did you honestly think something like that would dishearten me?!" Elzard screeched, unleashing another onslaught of lightning. "If that's a magic item, it has a limit to how much it can absorb, right?! I'll just beat the crap out of it until it breaks! Go ahead! Savor it!"

She was right. Even the Armor of the Demon Lord would break upon reaching its absorption point. Since it was facing lightning attacks cast by one of the fiercest warriors of the ancient world, it could withstand a maximum of a hundred spells, give or take.

That said, even if she managed to break the spear, it wasn't as if she could win against me.

Elzard continued to hurl her attacks. I flicked some flames in her direction to edge her closer to the end of her magical powers, but she must have taken my behavior as pessimism, because she sneered at me.

"Ha! C'mon, what's wrong?! You've gotta go on the offensive if you wanna win!" She rained down more bolts with a victorious look on her face.

Her idiocy made me loose-lipped. "Heh-heh... Elzard... For someone your age, you fight like a child," I mocked, chuckling to myself.

She was looking to issue some sort of rebuttal...

"Shouldn't you watch your step?" I suggested.

Elzard leaped to the side, landing on ground that erupted into a scorching firestorm. It was a combination of earth and fire magic known as *Ground Bomb*. I'd been steering her whereabouts for some time, and it had all been leading up to this.

"*U-uuuuuurg?!*" Elzard's screams rang out in the center of the scorching burst, and I sent an icy smile in her direction.

"You fight in the same manner as those who wield absolute power. There is a major drawback characteristic of those warriors, you know, which is that those who have never experienced difficult battles will only employ simple strategies on the battlefield. That makes you susceptible to falling for easy tricks. It seems like you learned nothing from when you had the rug pulled out from under you thousands of years ago."

The *Ground Bomb* disappeared as it reached its limit, but the single attack seemed to do significant damage. I glanced at her body, which was completely scorched and giving off smoke, as I held my spear at the ready.

"In my opinion, the strongest warriors don't employ enough caution. It must stem from the foolish delusion that there's no way they'll die or that victory is as good as theirs... And it seems to me that you're still convinced you're going to win, even now. Let me tell you something."

I focused my strength into the spear in my hand.

"There is nothing in this world that cannot be destroyed."

I aimed the crimson spear at Elzard, propelling it through space before it pierced my target straight through her chest. Its momentum yanked her entire body backward, drawing her toward the edge of the summit. Her gash spewed fresh blood until she finally plummeted into the sea of clouds spread out below us.

"*Aaaaaaaaaaaaaaaaaaaaaaaarddddddddddd!*" shouted Ireena as she jumped on me. "I—I knew you'd win! But still! I was so worried! I'm so happy you won! Thank goodness you're not hurt! I'm so relieeeeeeeeeved!"

I guessed this battle had made it hard for even Ireena to have absolute faith in me.

As enormous globs of tears fell from her eyes, she celebrated my victory, and I held on to her tightly, stroking her head.

Whew, Ireena was the best of the best.

"Th-this is a dream...! It's a nightmare! That must be it...!"

"Really? The King of Dragons fell...just like that...?!"

The demons were crestfallen, not that there was any need to consider their feelings.

Everything had finally come to a close. *We'll return to the capital and enjoy a nice meal together*, I thought when I saw something squirming below the summit in the sea of clouds in the distance.

In the next instant, milky-white clouds grew dark as thunder boomed through the sky.

A bright flash shot up toward outer space.

"*Aaaaaaaaaaaaargh! Aaaaaaaaard! Meteooooooooor!*" it roared with enough force to shake the earth before it finally made its appearance, piercing through the clouds and flying through the air.

It was a gigantic three-winged white dragon—a majestic sight deserving of the title of the Frenzied King of Dragons.

"*Not yet! This isn't oveeeeeeeeeer yet!*" she shrieked furiously just as a golden magic circle burst out in front of the true form of Elzard.

"Well, well... Don't you know that no one likes persistent women?" I asked, knitting my eyebrows together as I used every ounce of power to mentally construct a special-class defense spell.

It was complete within seconds, and I cast this spell even as it was still consuming my magical energy, covering Ireena and me in a thick golden membrane with a radius of about fifty merel.

I set a seven-circle defense spell of the highest caliber, *Ultima Wall*, in place—just in the nick of time.

"*Disappeaaaaaaaaaar!*" Elzard roared, launching off another spell and shooting a thick beam of blue light with enough strength to knock down a castle or two.

But my defensive barrier wasn't some ordinary spell, either. It was steely enough that your run-of-the-mill dragon wouldn't manage to lay a scratch on it. That said, it seemed Elzard wasn't your average beast, since the first of my seven layers was pulverized upon her attack's impact.

A horde of demons stood within the trajectory of her assault.

"*Eeeeeeeeeek?!*" one of them shrieked.

But I didn't have enough mental capacity to deal with them. I observed the demons get swallowed up by the beams and disappear as I thought to myself:

...After this damn lizard was defeated a thousand years ago, I bet she holed up on this summit for a millennium. And since mana, or magical energy, concentrates heavily in areas closer to outer space, I guess the magical density on this mountain wouldn't be too different from my time. If she spent her years here, that means...

"*Raaaaaaaaaaaaaaaaaaaaaaaaaaaaaaaagh!*"

That meant Elzard's magic had been spared any and all deterioration through the eras.

The second beam came whizzing toward us and took more than one demon with it before it chewed through another one of my defensive barriers. Five layers left.

...I guess I expected it would come down to this. I swear I have the shittiest luck.

"Ireena," I said in a tone of resignation as I peered into her face.

It displayed a look of worry—and fear. But I could see there was also trust: *Ard will think of something.* And that had given her hope.

Ireena, I'll protect you no matter what.

It didn't matter what would happen as a result. As long as she was alive, that was enough.

I believed this from the bottom of my heart…but I still couldn't stop my heart from overflowing with emotion and spilling out some words of its own.

"I implore you not to watch this upcoming battle."

I could tell she noticed that my heart was shattering based on my tone of voice, and she looked at me quizzically. But there was nothing more I could say.

I was going to throw off my mask, my identity as Ard Meteor, to become the Demon Lord Varvatos once more.

All roads lead to despair.

That is the way of life for a pitiful man.

I began the incantation of my greatest and strongest magic made exclusively for my personal use, an *Original*.

In complete solitude is he.

For there are those who follow his lead

But none to rule together with him.

Two of the remaining five layers were ground down.

"*Ha-ha-ha-ha-ha! Suffer! Ard Meteooooooor!*" bellowed Elzard, causing Ireena's face to cloud over in intense fear.

I gripped Ireena tightly in my arms as reassurance, continuing with my chanting.

There is not one who understands.

All are eager to leave his side.

One layer remaining. And I was this close to finishing my incantation.

Cast away by his one and only friend,

He sinks into a sea of madness and isolation.

The final layer was crushed under the weight of her attack. Elzard was raring to deliver her finishing blow, summoning another magic circle.

Rest without peace.
Drown in anguish and despair.
That which guides this tale.

Private Kingdom—the story of a lonely king.

As the chant came to a close, it invoked the appearance of a certain figure. We were surrounded by countless magic circles that flashed in and out of existence until they finally revealed one woman.

She was stunning—drop-dead gorgeous. With long silver hair that brushed past her hips and pointed ears, she exhibited a mature loveliness. Her beauty was timeless.

Her entire body was bound in a pitch-black straitjacket...

THREAT DETECTED: LEVEL III.

RELEASING CONSTRAINTS BY 15 PERCENT.

INITIATING DEFENSE MANEUVERS.

A robotic voice echoed out of her as she ripped off the bonds on her right hand, her facade as emotionless as a puppet. In the next moment, Elzard shot out another blast of light in our direction, and the summoned held out her palm in the face of the oncoming deluge.

A direct hit.

But when her attack made contact with the woman's fingertips, it completely absorbed its power.

"What is she...?!"

I had no obligation to answer that question.

I was ready to take it to the next level.

As I drew near the woman, her face twitched slightly, turning to look at me. There was something about her face that reminded me a little of Ireena, but those blue eyes held no emotion in them at all.

Well, she was nothing but a doll—nothing but a pitiful puppet my soul had captured.

I called out to her. "...It's been a while. Shall we dance, *Lydia*?"

YES, MY LORD, she replied, bursting through all her restraints and embracing my body.

In the next moment, Lydia was enveloped in a blinding glow as she shape-shifted into a glistening liquid form. She coiled around the entire length of my right arm and transformed into a chain as black as midnight, which wound down to my fingertips where a giant sword of the same color appeared before me.

I softly stroked the woman-turned-weapon and fixed my eyes on Elzard to deliver a fierce glare.

I made a declaration. "I'll fight in your arena. Come, you lowly fool," I spat as I composed and activated a spell to float through the air.

Moments later, I was soaring high through the sky.

"Really? You're challenging a dragon to a battle in the air? I'll have you repent for your arrogance—with death! Recognize your power-lessness and despair!" Elzard boomed, expanding and beating her three enormous wings to hunt me down.

We faced each other on the threshold between earth and space.

"You keep yapping on about 'despair this' and 'despair that'…but I'm guessing you don't have a clue as to what you're saying. You know, you're a thousand years too young to be talking to me like that."

Looking down at my enemy, I spoke with icy indifference.

"Allow me to show you true despair (as the Demon Lord)."

I let my lips rise up into a snarl, causing Elzard to jump out of her skin, but she managed to recover immediately, regaining her spirit.

"Teach me if you can!" she yelled, unleashing the full range of her raging emotions.

We were about to begin our battle in the air—fighting it out in the dragon's home field.

The number of demons had greatly dwindled at the hands of Elzard, the white dragon. But they hadn't been completely eliminated, since they were able to recover with healing capabilities unique to demonkind. They'd even managed to heal from the injuries inflicted by Ard Meteor.

What was their next move?

The answer was obvious. They needed to fulfill their mission. If they swooped down on their sacrifice—Ireena, who was defenseless and exposed—they could dip out of this place and move forward with the ceremony.

All surviving demons knew this. But they couldn't move an inch.

Even though they perfectly understood what they needed to do, they couldn't actually carry it out—thanks to the scene before them.

"What is that…?!"

"I-is this real life…?!"

"To think we'd be fighting against that thing…!"

The ancient legends were being reenacted in front of them, in this very world.

Under a darkened sky, two combatants in black and white clashed violently against each other. Just as the demons thought a flash of red sliced through the air, a blue undulation would fill the sky—back and forth, colors streaked through space without end. In the midst of these bursts of red and blue, there were flares of black and white that zigzagged through the sky.

The demons had no idea what the two were doing out there.

This entire battle was beyond their understanding, even though they were known as the scourge of society.

But they were certain about one thing: They were puny compared to the two figures in the sky. It was the one thing of which everyone was painfully aware.

The demons noticed that they'd fallen to their knees, clasping their hands.

"Ah...! Ah...!"

"Please forgive us...! Oh, please...!"

They begged through rattling teeth and full-body convulsions. Their hearts had been seized by absolute awe and terror. This was how anyone would react in the face of near-omnipotent beings and an incomprehensible situation.

The demons shed themselves of all other thought as they focused on offering their prayers, no longer strapped to a sense of duty or loyalty toward their master.

Their hearts had been completely pulverized by the sight of these two monsters and the pure terror they'd inflicted on each and every one of them.

Next to the demons panicking to raise their prayers in despair was Ireena, the elf, who was trembling uncontrollably. The shock waves of the monstrous blows from up above washed over her as she mumbled to herself.

"This is what it looks like for Ard to go all out...!"

Calling him *phenomenal* or *irregular* wasn't nearly enough: He was moving at a speed almost as fast as light. Any one of his attacks could level an entire city in one critical hit.

But he acted as if he'd done it his whole life. He was in the realm of the gods. The world of mortals was far below him.

This was why Ireena couldn't help thinking, *He scares me.*

...It meant she hadn't known anything about Ard; she'd only thought she knew him. But now, Ireena had figured out his true identity—all too well.

In truth, it made her want to draw a line between them—with her as a god-fearing worshipper and him as a deity. Ireena was at a crossroads: She was beginning to find it difficult to see the two of them as equals. She was about to join the demons in clasping her hands in prayer. Her heart creaked under the weight of her distress.

But she caught herself in the nick of time. "What am I thinking?!" Ireena puffed out both her cheeks and returned to her senses.

Ard's parting words came to mind: He'd implored her not to watch their duel. He must have been afraid Ireena would distance herself if she saw his true powers. Which meant they were one and the same.

"When Ard found out my secret…he said we were still friends…!" *I need to follow suit and think of our friendship as a lifelong one.* Making him sad was the last thing she wanted.

Ireena glared at the sky above her, where the battle was playing out in the heavens, clenching her fists tightly. She was going to etch this moment into her mind as her goal—her destination and desire.

"I'll stand there someday, too…and we'll walk as equals, shoulder to shoulder. And then," she said, stopping for a moment.

And then, I'll stop being scared of you. I'll dispel these newly formed thoughts, and then we finally can be true friends.

"Just you wait, Ard…!" Ireena shouted, full of determination, as she continued gazing up at her precious friend.

◇◆◇

MAGICAL ENERGY DETECTED FROM BELOW.

POSSIBILITY OF MAGIC CIRLE FORMING IN 0.2 SECONDS: VERY HIGH.

As soon as the robotic voice emitted out of my dark sword, I turned my focus to what was underneath me, and true to her word, a golden circle appeared two-tenths of a second later, emitting a wide beam of blue light.

It would have been a direct hit if my battle support unit hadn't given me an advance warning. But thanks to her insight, I was able to deal with it accordingly, swinging down my sword at the heat rays emanating unparalleled evil. The tip of the violent torrent made contact with my blade, which absorbed Elzard's magic until the light disappeared. I felt my magical energy replenishing.

This was just one of the many abilities of my exclusive spell: Soak up my opponent's attacks and transfuse their power into me. That meant I wouldn't run out of energy as long as I wasn't casting some gigantic spell that could consume all my magical power.

I raced through the darkness with Elzard.

ELEVATED HEAT DETECTED FROM THE LEFT AND RIGHT SIDES.

ANTICIPATE DIRECT IMPACT IN 3 SECONDS ON CURRENT TRAJECTORY.

"Construct a magical formula to accelerate. Plan for a counterattack after our escape," I ordered.

YES, MY LORD.

LOADING TECHNIQUE FOR ACCELERATION. PLEASE STAND BY...

CONSTRUCTION COMPLETE. ACCELERATING.

I could feel an immense force being pressed on my entire body a moment later, pushing me forward at the speed of light.

Three seconds passed before two rays seemed to collide behind me, assailing me with a heat wave—super far from hitting its target, me. As I experienced the scorching blaze surrounding my whole body, I constructed another technique together with Lydia.

"Lydia. Code Alpha. Ready."

UNDERSTOOD.

LOADING EXECUTIONER RAY. PLEASE STAND BY...

COMPLETE. READY TO FIRE.

As soon as my magical energy combusted, it manifested a bunch of magic circles before me—666, to be exact.

Each enormous circle blasted bloodred flashes of light, which accumulated into thousands of beams that hounded Elzard. But she moved with a litheness that belied her size.

"Slow, slow, way too slow!" she mocked, beating her gigantic wings.

Elzard sailed through the sky, evading a few beams, neutralizing some others, and knocking them away one by one. But she couldn't handle them all, and a hundred torrents of light hit her directly.

And the damage wasn't negligible: She'd lost two of her three wings. Her left arm was torn to shreds, and all that was left was a stump. There was a hole in her ribs that whistled when the wind rushed through it.

That said, these wounds were nothing for someone from ancient times. In fact, Elzard regenerated her entire body in the blink of an eye, fully recovering in no time at all.

"Ha-ha! I was wondering what might happen when we started …but it turns out this is no biggie! Your exclusive spells are nothing but weak copies of the species-specific abilities of white dragons!" she noted triumphantly.

Elzard must have already assumed she'd won this one.

"We can heal our injuries by taking in the magical energy in the atmosphere. But you, on the other hand, need to absorb it from your enemy. Your healing method is second-rate, obviously. Well, it seems to strengthen your baseline abilities, which isn't too shabby…but it lacks the firepower to take down this form."

She was right. As things were, it just wasn't enough, which meant I couldn't defeat Elzard.

There were a few moments at the outset when she'd been cornered into dangerous situations, which had contributed to her nerves at the very beginning of the fight. But now that she was secure in her victory, she was intoxicated with relief. That's why she could talk as if everything had already been decided.

"You'll be much happier dying here, y'know? …It seems like

you're hoping for Ireena to do something down there, but that's all moot. Sure, she's a monster, too, but she's leagues below you. Just because you're cut from the same cloth doesn't guarantee you'll stay friends. Once she knows the unabridged truth, she'll grow to fear... and betray you," Elzard continued. "There's no place for friendship or love in this world."

I felt a heaviness weigh me down when she delivered that last line. It was true.

Ireena is going to be horrified. I bet our relationship is already done for, I thought, causing my heart to cloud over and go dark.

Elzard snorted mockingly. "Solitude is your burden to carry. Perish with it in your arms. That's the perfect ending for someone like—"

Her hateful tirade was cut off by a voice that reached my ears.

"You can do ittttttt! Arrrrrrrrrrrrrrrd!" cheered Ireena.

She did sound a bit frightened, but her words were filled with platonic love.

"Go get 'er! You're not allowed to loooooooooose!"

Come back. Come back to me in one piece. It was as if I could hear her thoughts...and I felt my own eyes grow misty with tears.

I shifted my attention to Elzard floating across from me, flashing her a placid smile. "You've got one thing wrong... I'm not alone anymore."

She expressed her displeasure. "Is that so?! Lemme tell you: There's no point to any of this if you're dead!" she spewed, manifesting five enormous magic circles in front of her.

I glared her down. "Well. The preparations are done. Guess we can start," I said before I turned to give Lydia an order—one that would offer this stupid, cocky dragon in front of me a true taste of despair.

"Lydia. Phase II. Ready."

UNDERSTOOD.

SWITCHING TO STAGE II OF FULL-BODY TRANSFORMATION.

ACTIVATING BRAVE DEMON.

In perfect synchronicity with this reply, the chain on my right arm started to release a black aura, seeping out and cloaking my entire body to begin the transformation. The clothes on my back turned into a pitch-black costume, and my hair drained of all color into a sinister, pure white.

"Ha! You just look a li'l different is all! What is that gonna do?!" Elzard yelled back in her ever-confident tone as she cast another spell.

Five golden circles emanated a blinding glow as they appeared in front of Elzard's eyes.

ANALYSIS COMPLETE.

INITIATING MAGIC CANCELER.

A mechanical voice came out from the sword...and the five circles crumbled, scattering their contents everywhere.

"What?!" Elzard shrieked, appearing totally at a loss as to what had just happened.

That said, her usual fervor immediately came back, and she managed to manifest another set of magic circles.

"*It's over, Ard Meteor!*" she shouted as if issuing a command, unleashing another spell on me.

But her azure pillars of light didn't go off in my direction—but in hers.

"—Ngh!"

A surprise attack within a surprise attack. This was something even Elzard couldn't dodge—resulting in multiple direct hits and leaving her with five wide gashes.

"Wh-what is this...? What's going on...?!" she asked, completely bewildered.

I revealed a few of my secrets. "You spoke disparagingly about my exclusive spells, but you should know that absorbing magical energy is a small part of a bigger story. The main capacity of this form of magic is in...analysis and control."

"Analysis and control...?!" parroted Elzard as she healed herself.

I nodded at my enemy. "Aye. In this form, I can analyze my enemy's moves. And when that's complete, it's possible for me to take over. But it's not just about letting your spells run amok. I can unlock any and all methods you've employed to conceal your magical techniques. Once I take a look at your arsenal of secret skills in there, I can copy and make them mine. That is to say—" I paused, swinging my black sword to point its tip at her and smiling assuredly. "All your attacks are mine. You cannot win."

Elzard's entire body jolted, even though her expression hadn't changed. But I could tell despair was beginning to take root in her heart.

Not that it hurt to be sure.

"These *Originals* will continue to metamorphose as I fuse more and more of my body with the soul of my dear friend. And I've got two more forms left. I'm assuming you know what this all means, right?"

At that, Elzard's body began to tremble all over. "*G-graaaaa aaaaagh!*" she howled as seven magic circles spread out before her, set to release more torrents of light.

"I told you that wouldn't work," I warned calmly, taking control of her spell to pierce her with her own attacks once again.

"*Graaaaaaaaaaagh!* Th-this......this can't be happening...!" she screeched, riddled with seven enormous holes that rained down profuse amounts of fresh blood.

She cried out in anguish.

I smiled twistedly. "What do you think? This is what you'd call 'true despair'—the moment a certain victory is completely flipped on its head. It's when you experience the most extreme shift in emotions, from astronomical relief to absolute misery. I wish I could spend more time teaching you about yourself...but this all ends here," I lamented, thrusting the tip of my sword before her.

"To the King of Dragons and the frenzied madman. May you die in despair."

Elzard unleashed the full extent of her wrath on me as she continued to regenerate her body. *"Don't screw with meeeeeeeee! The only one dying here is youuuuu!"*

At the eleventh hour, she began a truly useless struggle.

"Fourme. Evisa. Gwyneth... Analyze these if you can!" she challenged, chanting three incantations in the language of dragons.

They called forward a ginormous magic circle more than a hundred merel in diameter.

...Huh. This technique is too high-level for me to analyze at my current stage.

"I have no need to analyze it. I'll just crush it head-on," I remarked, face plastered with an unchanging grin. I gave Lydia an order. "Code Sigma. Ready."

UNDERSTOOD.

ULTIMATUM ZERO. PLEASE STAND BY.

With that, seven titanic magic circles manifested and overlapped before me.

CHARGING MAGICAL ENERGY. 30 PERCENT... 40 PERCENT... 50 PERCENT...

They began to spin around, reverberating a dull sound similar to the chimes of a large bell.

"Evsim, Lufasa, Urvis, Azura...," chanted Elzard, creating and rotating magic circles of her own.

A high-pitched *shillling* resounded through the air.

CHARGING MAGICAL ENERGY. EXCEEDING 70 PERCENT.

As our circles made a series of cacophonous noises, we stared each other down.

80 PERCENT... 90 PERCENT... MAGICAL ENERGY HAS ACHIEVED 100 PERCENT.

The dragon had spewed out the last of her chant at the exact same time.

"*Disappear! ELDER BREATH!*" she shrieked as the giant golden circle sparkled with a conspicuously strong light—

READY TO FIRE AT ANY TIME. HOW SHALL I PROCEED?

"Guess it's go time. *Ultimatum Zero*, fire."

A wave of blue light cascaded over the edges of the golden magic circle as a red luminescence gushed out of the black ones—unleashing their glowing floods in an explosive power akin to a bomb detonation. The two streams of light collided between us, fiercely pushing each other forward and back and unleashing a blinding flash and shock wave upon impact.

They contained enough kinetic force to make a few laps around the planet, causing my silver hair to whip back violently. The struggle lasted for a full thirty seconds before finally beginning to break down.

My crimson beam began overwhelming the blue lights.

"*R-ridiculous! Are you freaking kidding meeeeeee?!*"

The body of the colossal dragon vanished as it screeched in total anguish.

The red torrent would shoot through space, reaching its limit and gradually growing narrower—until the very last red particle was finally extinguished, leaving behind nothing at all.

Or so I'd thought.

"...Oh my. That was unexpected."

I was the tiniest bit surprised by the sight before me.

I'd had no intention of making any allowances, casting my *Ultimatum Zero* in full force.

But even after my target had been fully immersed in my attack, Elzard was still alive. I guess I should've expected that from a dragon from the legends. No one else had ever survived this before. Even if my

trump card was weaker than it had been in my heyday, the fact that she'd lived through it was worthy of praise.

"Ggh... U-ugh...," she stammered, body covered in wounds.

Elzard had lost 60 percent of her body, which she couldn't regenerate. I assumed she'd used up most of her magical energy with that last bold move, and she was barely hanging on to her life, which was as capricious as flickering candlelight in the wind.

I reached out to reap it.

"Am I going to die...? Will I die as alone...as I was in life...?" she whispered fraily.

My final blow wavered upon hearing her dying words, which revealed her truest self—bottomless sorrow and loneliness. My resolve dulled for an instant.

"No...! I won't die, damn it...! I'll kill you...! Kill you till you're worse than dead...!" howled the white dragon, overflowing with a thirst for blood.

I finally snapped back to my senses.

But it was already too late. Before the knockout blow could land, the enemy made her move.

Elzard's body grew transparent. Had she cast...a reincarnation spell?

To test out this theory, I cast *Flare*, but the flames passed right through her body without any effect whatsoever.

"Ard Meteor...! To me, you're—"

But she completely disappeared before she could finish.

"...As if a child on the verge of tears," I noted upon seeing the grief and desolation in those golden eyes as she took her leave.

Elzard had been historically known as a fearsome monster who'd annihilated the country and betrayed the woman who'd become her friend. But I had a hard time seeing her as just a beast, and somewhere deep down, I had a feeling we were very much alike.

...Welp, thinking about it now isn't gonna change anything.

I glanced at the black sword gripped in my right hand. "Lydia. You served admirably. You may return inside my soul."

YES, MY LORD.

The dark sword and chain on my arm dissolved into smoke, coiling in the air and vanishing as my body assumed its original appearance—my guise as Ard Meteor. I descended to the summit below, where I spotted Ireena.

When she saw me, her body jerked.

...Ah, I knew it would turn out like this. She must have seen that last attack, *Ultimatum Zero*, and changed her mind about the whole thing. Her heart must be broken, which meant the girl who'd been cheering me on was nowhere to be seen.

Whatever. I was used to being alone. And I'd been able to protect her—unlike Lydia.

That was enough—

"W-wowie, I knew you were amazing, Ard!" Ireena chirped, slicing through all my thoughts.

She locked eyes with me, and I could see fear...and determination behind her gaze.

"Just as I'd expect from my *friend*! But don't think I'm always gonna be weaker than you! I'll get lots stronger, then..." She collected her thoughts.

"I'll be a girl you can depend on. No question."

The corners of my eyes grew hot.

Ha-ha. I'm so stupid. How could I think Ireena would ever abandon me?

After all, this girl was kinder than anyone.

I swiped at the tears pooling in the outer edges of my eyes. "Ireena...will you continue to be my friend?"

"Duh! I can't wait to spend more time with you going forward, Ard!"

We shook hands, just like when we first met.

I smiled shyly at her, and Ireena flashed the pure, innocent grin of a child.

I'd finally escaped from loneliness, thousands of years in the future.

"—By the way, Ireena. You held out your left hand again, didn't you?"

"Ah! S-sorry! I—I didn't mean anything by iiiiiiit!"

There was a lot that happened, but for now, I'll close with this: *Ireena is seriously the cutest!*

CHAPTER 21
The Ex–Demon Lord and a Change in Scenery

With the incident at hand coming to a close, Weiss the Heroic Baron and the Great Mages—Jack and Carla—headed home to their village, swaying in a horse-drawn carriage as it trotted forward.

"In any case, this whole thing seems fishy," Jack noted.

"I know, totally! There's a bunch of red flags," Carla replied, as skeptical as her husband about the entire situation.

Weiss nodded. "I agree. It's odd that this incident happened at all."

There were two reasons for this.

One: It was unclear how the identities of Weiss and Ireena were leaked, especially because fewer than ten people had been aware that the pair carried the bloodline of the Evil Gods. Of those privileged with this knowledge, there was virtually no chance that anybody was conspiring with the demons. They were all at a total loss as to how this information got out.

Two: The sum total of demons at the scene gave them pause. With their species low in number, they'd never been able to execute anything other than a few small-scale attacks. Even in that incident when an Evil God had been revived ten years prior, the demons had achieved their goal through a series of smaller events.

This most recent occurrence was the largest in known history.

But the demon casualties numbered in the thousands. With these losses, Lars al Ghoul had to be on the brink of annihilation. It made sense if they were going all out after betting every last chip on this one plan…

But it wouldn't make sense, since the top brass of the organization—not to mention their leader—hadn't been at the scene. That meant this abduction incident hadn't been the final act. This wasn't over.

Then, why would the demons try to pull off a plan that would result in major casualties? Especially when they didn't have many of their kin to begin with?

There was no reasonable answer to this, which made it even more shrouded in mystery.

"…I imagine Ireena will continue to face dangerous situations day in and day out."

"Yep, it looks that way. But no need to worry. I mean, c'mon," Jack replied.

"Ireena has our boy with her, after all!" Carla crooned.

They were absolutely convinced that her safety was guaranteed.

Weiss agreed. "You're right. Everything will be fine when he's by her side. That said…I wonder what he'll do when he discovers *our other secret*. Everything hinges on that," he murmured, flipping open a book that he'd brought to pass the time.

It was a timeless bestseller, the heroic ballad of the Demon Lord. Weiss had volume 98 out of 215 in his hands. This one was most famous for its tragedy.

"With his own hand, the Demon Lord murdered his close friend—Lydia the Champion. According to the tale, it's because Lydia was a traitor, but…the truth behind his motives isn't clear."

It was the biggest unsolved mystery of all time. Scholars were still debating it among themselves.

"We must hide the fact that we are kin with the Evil Gods—and the *descendants* of the former Champion, *Lydia*. Especially from Ard… I mean, from *the Demon Lord*."

Jack and Carla nodded in quiet contemplation.

The three of them had known that Ard Meteor was the reincarnated form of the Demon Lord just as he started to display a fraction of his true potential. There were several reasons.

One: It was incredibly strange that Ard had been born in the first place.

True, Jack and Carla may have been husband and wife, but they would never, ever, ever engage in any behavior that might result in bearing a child.

That's because they both preferred members of the same sex.

Which meant that when Carla became pregnant, they had their suspicions—which were confirmed once Ard showed multiple instances of lacking common sense during his time in the village.

"…Going back to the day when she met Ard. Ireena went on a rare outing into the woods. She said she felt fate calling her there… It made sense. The moment I saw him, I sensed that our destinies were intertwined." Weiss sighed.

Would it lead them toward happiness…or disaster—following their ancestral paths?

The two Great Mages were as uncertain as Weiss.

"It might wind up not bein' such a big deal."

"But if he's been traumatized by any chance…"

"Their friendship would fall apart when he projects the image of Lydia on Ireena."

The three sighed collectively. Ard and Ireena had a difficult journey ahead. It would be ideal if the truth could be hidden forever, but that would be too difficult.

That's because all secrets eventually come to light.

Ireena's abduction brought a slew of changes to my surroundings in its aftermath.

First and foremost, Operation: Instructor Ard.

I'd received high praise for Ireena's rescue and been granted a part-time teaching position as both student and instructor. Why...?

There was one other major change regarding my living arrangements.

It was clear that intel about Ireena's identity had been leaked to the enemy, which meant she was in danger day in and day out. She needed a guard at all times, and the duty fell to me.

When it was decided that we'd live together, they prepared a two-person room in the dormitory for the aristocrats, making a special allowance for me to live there as a commoner. Our assigned room was unnecessarily huge. The floor had a luxurious red carpet and a big canopied bed in the center of the room.

It was worlds apart from the dorms of the commoners.

That aside.

On this day, we'd finished our supper, and it was time to wash up. There was a communal bathhouse annexed to the dormitory, but it was separated by gender, which meant it would force me to leave Ireena alone for a long period of time. Just to be safe, we decided to make do with the shower in the room.

"Phew... That felt amazing!" Ireena exclaimed as she stepped out of the shower wearing a single bath towel.

Which meant there was only a measly little veil covering up her two weapons of mass destruction. Not that she seemed too concerned about this whole thing...

Strange. My face feels kind of hot. But it's not like I'm feeling shy or embarrassed.

It could be because our bond had grown deeper just a few days prior. That was why I...

Nope. Let's leave it at that. I wouldn't get ahead of myself.

I enjoyed chatting for a while with Ireena, who'd slipped into her negligee right in front of me and…who I would be sharing a bed with once again.

Why is there only one bed in the room? I'd sent in an immediate request for a second one.

"It's totally fine, right? We'll just keep it this way! I wanna sleep with you every night, Ard!" she exclaimed innocently, which made it impossible to refuse her wishes.

"W-well then, I suppose we ought to get to sleep."

"Right!" she chirped, nodding happily.

Ireena settled in and lay down beside me like it was totally normal, as if a puppy cuddling up to sleep with her master.

Why do I feel nervous? Maybe I'm…

My train of thought was interrupted by a huge *BWAAAAAA AAAM!* and the thunderous echo that followed. We were both convinced it was an assassin, leaping to our feet…but we were wrong.

There was a large hole in the wall near the bed.

"Good evening, you two, ♪" sang Ginny, the succubus, smiling cheerfully.

It appeared she'd punched through the wall with her bare hands. She trotted over to us and perched herself on the bed.

"I'm actually going to be your neighbor from now on, so I thought I could make this into a three-person room. ♡ I'm looking forward to having you as roommates! ♡"

Ireena's face burned with rage as she snapped at the grinning gal. *"Q-q-quit screwing arouuuuuund!"*

"Oh, that's right, Ard! Remember my one-hundred-women harem plan? I've found some candidates, so I'll be sure to introduce you next time. ♪" Ginny ignored Ireena and all her fury.

"H-hold up. A one-hundred-women harem? What are you talking about?"

"Didn't you bring up the idea yourself? You want to make a

hundred friends, right? Which means you don't want to stop at a harem of five or six girls—but at an even one hundred."

Nope, you're totally off. I just want friends. I never said it was limited to girls.

I tried explaining this to her, but Ginny didn't seem to be listening at all.

"Hmm, this room is too small for that many girls. Let's all move to a huge mansion eventually! Don't worry! I'm sure you'll be able to buy one or two like it's nothing! And you can leave the selection of candidates to me!"

"Er, I'm not leaving you in charge of anything. I don't even want—"

"*I already told you—no haremsssss!*" Ireena screeched, forcing her way into the conversation and launching into a full-on argument with Ginny.

I smiled wryly as I watched from the sidelines.

"It seems life will still be anything but boring…"

AFTERWORD

To readers of my previous work, it's nice to see you again. As for new readers, it's nice to meet you. I'm Myojin Katou.

This work was originally serialized online on *Shousetsuka ni Narou*. This version has been edited from head to toe and become an actual book.

Well then, everyone, I'm going to change the topic. It's that time of year again.

Yep. It's *Monster Hunter* season.

I don't mean to go on and on about me, but I've been playing since the very first game. I've been too busy to keep up with most games, but that doesn't stop me from being a hardcore Hunter who's always up for some *Monster Hunter*. I'm that big of a fan.

(Time to sell myself.) Please bless me with work, Capcom.

That's why I've already logged 150 hours on the newest game, *Monster Hunter: World*, which went on sale on January 26. I know there was some discourse around changing the console for this game, but I'd been hoping it would come out on the PS4, so this was good news to me. Of course, the graphics are seriously amazing. And the middle-aged male character I customized looked really cool, super-cool, awesomely cool. Absolutely amazing.

...Huh? Female characters? What's that?

If I started talking about all the other great things about it, I could easily fill up a hundred pages—no joke. I'll cut it short this time.

On to a different subject.

The life of a novelist is a stressful one.

You confront your poor writing skills, or panic when you've hit writer's block, or get sick of hearing kids screaming in your neighborhood, or become depressed by projecting the sound of their innocent laughter onto your own childhood, or start to get pissed off when you overhear them living their day-to-day lives... Yeah, that sort of stress follows novelists around all the time.

I've lived the novelist life for only a year. It might be presumptuous of me to say this, but I sincerely believe that it's impossible to write when dealing with these major stressors.

And I think novelists should take it into their own hands to reduce them.

But I had a tough time implementing this myself and suffered as a consequence.

When I was writing this book, I was super stressed by the neighborhood kids. Just as I wondered what to do, I saw a beacon of hope.

On that fateful day, I was mindlessly watching television when *that* commercial came on. You know the one. Yep, it was for *Monster Hunter: World*, featuring the man who came closest to ruling Suzuran High, Takayuki Yamada.

Wow. It made an impact on me to see a grown man play make-believe, earnestly and passionately pretending to be in the *Monster Hunter* world. It was endearing and enviable.

And I guess that led me to pretend to be in *Monster Hunter*, too.

There I was, a grown man in his early thirties, sprinting around his room yelling *"Diabloooooos!"* and jumping up and down, screeching *"Plesiooooooth!"*

I screamed from the soul. I was looking like some backward abnormality, as my name might suggest in Japanese.

I'm sure the neighborhood kids heard it and that the senseless screams of a crazy old man scared the crap out of them. Serves 'em right.

Anyway. Pretending to be in *Monster Hunter* healed my heart. It relieved my stress to play the part of a monster and act all eccentric.

I'm gonna keep doing this from now on, I thought to myself.

But it all ended with my Dos Jagie impression.

"...What're you doing?"

My parents walked in. How cliché. It had to be my parents. What a trope.

I used to watch live streams on *Nico Live* where parents barged in on streamers, and I'd laugh my head off. Maybe this was karma.

My parents were frozen in place. I didn't move an inch... *I will never pretend to be in* Monster Hunter *again*, I promised to myself.

—Not.

It was all, in fact, a lie. I couldn't think of anything for the afterword, so I made stuff up. There's no way a grown man would scream *"Diablooooooos,"* right?

Ah-ha-ha-ha.

...Well, that leaves me with some words of gratitude.

First, I would like to acknowledge my editor. I caused you a lot of trouble. Please forgive me for being a slow learner.

To Sao Mizuno, who provided the illustrations, thank you very much. Ireena looks seriously adorable.

And to those who supported me on the Internet. It's thanks to you that a physical book was even possible. Thank you. Please look forward to my future work.

Finally, all the readers holding this book in your hands: You have my deepest gratitude.

Well then, I pray we'll meet again in Volume 2. I'll sign off here.

Myojin Katou